Free Stuff For Kids

Our Pledge

We have collected and examined the best free and up-to-a-dollar offers we could find. Each supplier in this book has promised to honor properly made requests for **single items** through **1997.** Though mistakes do happen, we are doing our best to make sure this book really works.

—*The Free Stuff Editors*

Meadowbrook Press
Distributed by Simon & Schuster
New York

MW00764584

The Free Stuff Editors

Director: Bruce Lansky
Editor: Melanie Mallon
Researcher: Melanie Mallon
Copyeditor: Kevin Frazzini
Production Manager: Amy Unger
Desktop Publishing Manager: Patrick Gross
Cover Design: Amy Unger

ISBN: 0-88166-250-X
Simon & Schuster Ordering # 0-671-57374-8

ISSN: 1056-9693
20th edition

© 1976, 1977, 1978, 1979, 1980, 1981, 1982, 1983, 1984, 1985, 1986, 1987, 1988, 1989, 1990, 1991, 1992, 1993, 1994, 1995, 1996, 1997 by Meadowbrook Creations

All rights reserved. No part of this book may be reproduced in any form without written permission from the publisher, except in the case of brief quotations embodied in critical articles and reviews. Suppliers' addresses may not be reproduced in any form.

Published by Meadowbrook Press, 18318 Minnetonka Boulevard, Deephaven, MN 55391.

BOOK TRADE DISTRIBUTION by Simon & Schuster, a division of Simon and Schuster, Inc., 1230 Avenue of the Americas, New York, NY 10020.

97 96   5 4 3 2 1

Printed in the United States of America

Contents

Thank You's

To Pat Blakely, Barbara Haislet, and Judith Hentges for creating and publishing the original *Rainbow Book*, proving that kids, parents, and teachers would respond enthusiastically to a source of free things by mail. They taught us the importance of carefully checking the quality of each item and doing our best to make sure that each and every request is satisfied.

Our heartfelt appreciation goes to hundreds of organizations and individuals for making this book possible. The suppliers and editors of this book have a common goal: to make it possible for kids to reach out and discover the world by themselves.

Read This First

About This Book

Free Stuff for Kids lists hundreds of items you can send away for. The Free Stuff Editors have examined every item and think each is among the best offers available. There are no trick offers—only safe, fun, and informative things you'll like!

This book is designed for kids who can read and write. The directions on the following pages explain exactly how to request an item. Read the instructions carefully so you know how to send a request. Making sure you've filled out a request correctly is easy—just complete the *Free Stuff for Kids* Checklist on page 8. Half the fun is using the book on your own. The other half is getting a real reward for your efforts!

Each year the Free Stuff Editors create a new edition of this book, taking out old items, inserting new ones, and changing addresses and prices. It is important for you to use an updated edition because the suppliers only honor properly made requests for single items for the **current** edition. If you use this edition after **1997,** your request will not be honored.

Reading Carefully

Read the descriptions of the offers carefully to find out exactly what you're getting. Here are some guidelines to help you know what you're sending for:

• A pamphlet is usually one sheet of paper folded over and printed on both sides.

• A booklet is usually larger than a pamphlet and contains more pages, but it's smaller than a book.

Following Directions

It's important to follow each supplier's directions. On one offer, you might need to use a postcard. On another offer, you might be asked to include money or a long self-addressed stamped envelope. If you do not follow the directions **exactly,** you might not get your request. Unless the directions tell you differently, ask for only **one** of anything you send for. Family or classroom members using the same book must send **separate** requests.

Sending Postcards

A postcard is a small card you can write on and send through the mail without an envelope. Many suppliers offering free items require you to send requests on postcards. Please do this. It saves them the time it takes to open many envelopes.

The post office sells postcards with preprinted postage. You can also buy postcards at a drugstore and put special postcard stamps on them yourself. Your local post office can tell you how much a postcard stamp currently costs. (Postcards with a picture on them are usually more expensive.) You must use a postcard that is at least 3½-by-5½ inches. (The post office will not take 3-by-5-inch index cards.) Your postcards should be addressed like the one below:

Amy Lyons
110 Deerwood
Conroe, TX 77303

The Chicago Bulls
Fan Mail
1901 West Madison
Chicago, IL 60612

Dear Sir or Madam:

Please send me a Chicago Bulls fan pack. Thank you very much.

Sincerely,
Amy Lyons
110 Deerwood
Conroe, TX 77303

Front   Back

- **Neatly print** the supplier's address on the side of the postcard that has the postage. Put your return address in the upper left-hand corner of that side as well.
- **Neatly print** your request, your name, and your address on the blank side of the pos...
- Do not abbreviate the name of your street or city.
- Use a ballpoint pen. Pencil can be difficult to read, and ink pens often smear.

Sending Letters

Your letters should look like the one below:

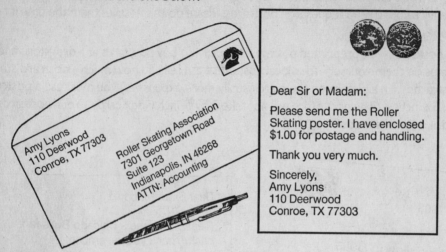

Dear Sir or Madam:

Please send me the Roller Skating poster. I have enclosed $1.00 for postage and handling.

Thank you very much.

Sincerely,
Amy Lyons
110 Deerwood
Conroe, TX 77303

Amy Lyons
110 Deerwood
Conroe, TX 77303

Roller Skating Association
7301 Georgetown Road
Suite 123
Indianapolis, IN 46268
ATTN: Accounting

- **Neatly print** the name of the item you want exactly as you see it in the directions.
- **Neatly print** your own name and address at the bottom of the letter. (Do not abbreviate the name of your street or city.)
- If you're including coins or a long self-addressed stamped envelope, say so in the letter. And be sure to enclose the coins and the envelope!
- Put a **first-class stamp** on any envelope you send. You can get stamps at the post office.
- **Neatly print** the supplier's address in the center of the envelope and your return address in the upper left-hand corner.

ou're sending many letters at once, make sure you put the correct letter in the correct envelope.

ballpoint pen. Pencil can be difficult to read, and ink pens often smear.

Sending a Long Self-Addressed Stamped Envelope

If the directions say to enclose a long self-addressed stamped envelope, here's how to do it:

• **Neatly print** your name and address in the center of a **9½-inch-long envelope** as if you were mailing it to yourself. Print your return address in the upper left-hand corner of the envelope as well. Put a **first-class stamp** on it.

```
Amy Lyons
110 Deerwood
Conroe, TX 77303

                Amy Lyons
                110 Deerwood
                Conroe, TX 77303
```

• **Fold up** (but don't seal!) the long self-addressed stamped envelope, and put it inside another **9½-inch-long envelope** (along with your letter to the supplier). Put a **first-class stamp** on the second envelope, too.

• **Neatly print** the supplier's address in the center of the outside envelope and your return address in the upper left-hand corner.

• Use a ballpoint pen.

Sending Money

Many of the suppliers in this book are not charging you for their items. However, the cost of postage and handling is high today, and suppliers must charge you for this. If the directions say to enclose money, **you must do so.** Here are a few rules about sending money:

• Tape the coins to your letter or index card so they won't break out of the envelope.

• Don't stack your coins on top of each other in the envelope.

• Don't use pennies and avoid using nickels. These coins will add weight to your envelope, and you may need to use more than one stamp.

• If an item costs $1.00, send a one-dollar bill instead of coins. Don't tape dollar bills.

• Send only U.S. money.

• If a grown-up is helping you, he or she may write a check (unless the directions tell you not to send checks).

• Send all money directly to the suppliers—their addresses are listed with their offers.

Getting Your Stuff

Expect to wait **four to eight weeks** for your stuff to arrive. Sometimes you have to wait longer. Remember, suppliers get thousands of requests each year. Please be patient! If you wait a long time and your offer still doesn't come, you may be using the wrong edition. This is the **1997** edition—the offers in this book will only be good for 1996 and 1997!

Making Sure You Get Your Request

The Free Stuff Editors have tried to make the directions for using this book as clear as possible, to make sure you get what you send for. But you must follow **all** of the directions **exactly** as they're written, or the supplier **will not be able to answer your request.** If you're confused about the directions, ask a grown-up to help you.

Do's and Don'ts:

- **Do** use a ballpoint pen. Typing and using a computer are okay, too.
- **Do** print. Cursive can be difficult to read.
- **Do** print your name, address, and ZIP code clearly and fully on the postcard or on the envelope **and** on the letter you send—sometimes envelopes and letters get separated after they reach the supplier. Do not abbreviate anything except state names. Abbreviations can be confusing.
- **Do** send the correct amount of U.S. money, but don't use pennies.
- **Do** tape the coins to the letter you send them with. If you don't tape them, the coins might rip the envelope and fall out.
- **Do** use a **9½-inch-long** self-addressed stamped envelope when the instructions ask for a "long" envelope.

INSTRUCTIONS

- **Do not** use this **1997** edition **after** 1997.

- **Do not** ask for more than **one** of an item, unless the directions say you can.

- **Do not** stack coins in the envelope.

- **Do not** seal your long self-addressed stamped envelope. The suppliers need to be able to put the item you ordered in the envelope you send.

- **Do not** ask Meadowbrook Press to send you any of the items listed in the book unless you are ordering the Meadowbrook offers from page 80. The publishers of this book do not carry items belonging to other suppliers. They do not supply refunds, either.

Follow all the rules to avoid disappointment!

What to Do If You Aren't Satisfied:

If you have complaints about any offer, or if you don't receive the items you sent for within eight to ten weeks, contact the Free Stuff Editors. Before you complain, please reread the directions. Are you sure you followed them properly? Are you using this **1997** edition **after** 1997? (The offers in this book are only good for 1996 and 1997.) The Free Stuff Editors won't be able to send you the item, but they can make sure that any suppliers who don't fulfill requests are dropped from next year's *Free Stuff for Kids*. For **each** of your complaints you must tell us the name of the offer as it appears in the book, the page number of the offer, and the date you sent your request. Without this information, we may not be able to help you. We'd like to know which offers you like and what kind of new offers you'd like us to add to next year's edition. So don't be bashful—write us a letter. Send your complaints or suggestions to:

The Free Stuff Editors
Meadowbrook Press
18318 Minnetonka Boulevard
Deephaven, MN 55391

Free Stuff for Kids Checklist

Use this checklist each time you send out a request. It will help you follow directions **exactly** and prevent mistakes. Put a check mark in the box each time you complete a task—you can photocopy this page and use it again and again.

For all requests:
❏ I sent my request during either **1996** or **1997.**

When sending postcards and letters:
❏ I used a ballpoint pen.
❏ I printed neatly and carefully.
❏ I asked for the correct item (only one).
❏ I wrote to the correct supplier.
❏ I double-checked the supplier's address.

When sending postcards only:
❏ I put my return address on the postcard.
❏ I applied a postcard stamp (if the postage wasn't preprinted).

When sending letters only:
❏ I put my return address on the letter.
❏ I included a **9½-inch-long** self-addressed stamped envelope (if the directions asked for one).
❏ I included the correct amount of money (if the directions asked for money).
❏ I put my return address on the envelope.
❏ I applied a **first-class stamp.**

When sending a long self-addressed stamped envelope:
❏ I used a **9½-inch-long** envelope.
❏ I put my address on the front of the envelope.
❏ I put my return address in the upper left-hand corner of the envelope.
❏ I left the envelope unsealed.
❏ I applied a **first-class stamp.**

When responding to one-dollar offers:
❏ I sent U.S. money.
❏ I enclosed a one-dollar bill with my letter instead of coins.

When sending coins:
❏ I sent U.S. money.
❏ I taped the coins to my letter or to an index card.
❏ I did not stack the coins on top of each other.
❏ I did not use pennies. (Extra coins make the envelope heavier and may require extra postage.)

MEADOWBROOK PRESS 1997 EDITION

U.S. MAIL

Sports

Home on the Rangers

You don't have to be in their new ballpark to root for the Rangers. Send for their schedule, souvenir list, and sticker to cheer like crazy, in or out of the ballpark.

Directions:	Read and follow the instructions on pages 2-8. **Print** your request **neatly** on paper and put it in an envelope. You must enclose a **long self-addressed stamped envelope.**
Write to:	Texas Rangers Souvenir Department P.O. Box 90111 Arlington, TX 76004-3111
Ask for:	Texas Rangers schedule, sticker, and souvenir list

Phillie Phanatics

Phreak out for the Philadelphia Phillies with this phabulous offer! Their fan pack is jammed full of fun items: two player photocards, pocket schedule, and team photo. You can also receive a special Phillie Phanatic photocard upon request.

Directions:	Read and follow the instructions on pages 2-8. **Print** your request **neatly** on paper and put it in an envelope. You must enclose a **long self-addressed stamped envelope.**
Write to:	Phillies Fan Mail P.O. Box 7575 Philadelphia, PA 19101
Ask for:	Schedule, two photocards, and team photo (*Phillie Phanatic photocard upon request*)

Twins Treats

You'll want to take this offer all the way home! The Minnesota Twins have a fan pack for baseball lovers everywhere. You'll receive a team and player photo, pocket schedule, novelty brochure, and sticker.

Directions:	Read and follow the instructions on pages 2-8. **Print** your request **neatly** on paper and put it in an envelope. You must enclose a **long self-addressed stamped envelope.**
Write to:	Attn: Fan Mail Minnesota Twins 501 Chicago Avenue South Minneapolis, MN 55415
Ask for:	Minnesota Twins pocket schedule, novelty brochure, sticker, and team/player photo

Tigerrific

Bring out the Tiger in you with this fan pack that's anything but tame. The Detroit Tigers will send you a logo sticker, schedule, roster, fact sheet, and a player photo.

Directions:	Read and follow the instructions on pages 2-8. **Print** your request **neatly** on paper and put it in an envelope. You must enclose a **long self-addressed stamped envelope.**
Write to:	Fan Pack Detroit Tigers 2121 Trumbull Detroit, MI 48216
Ask for:	Detroit Tigers fan pack

Astro Blast

Support the Houston Astros as they soar through another season. Ask for their special fan pack and you'll receive a ton of cool stuff: a player photo, logo sticker, and schedule.

Directions:	**Read and follow the instructions on pages 2-8. Print** your request **neatly** on paper and put it in an envelope. You must enclose a **long self-addressed stamped envelope.**
Write to:	Astros Fan Mail P.O. Box 288 Houston, TX 77001-0288
Ask for:	Astros schedule, logo sticker, and player photo

Mud Hen Mania

Whether you're from Toledo or Timbuktu, you gotta love a team with a mascot like Muddy the Mud Hen. And you're really gonna love the fun stuff Muddy has especially for you: a sticker, Muddy baseball cards, a pocket schedule, and even a note directly from Muddy to you!

Directions:	Read and follow the instructions on pages 2-8. Print your request neatly on paper and put it in an envelope. You must enclose a long self-addressed stamped envelope.
Write to:	Mud Hens Free Stuff Toledo Mud Hens 2901 Key Street Maumee, OH 43537
Ask for:	Mud Hens logo sticker, Muddy baseball cards, pocket schedule, and note from Muddy

The Grand Cannons

Get fired up for this offer from the mighty minor league. The Prince William Cannons have a cool new logo that you can collect when you send for their sticker, schedule, and souvenir list.

Directions:	Read and follow the instructions on pages 2-8. **Print** your request **neatly** on paper and put it in an envelope. You must enclose a **long self-addressed stamped envelope.**
Write to:	Prince William Cannons c/o Cannons Fan Pack P.O. Box 2148 Woodbridge, VA 22193
Ask for:	Prince William Cannons sticker, schedule, and souvenir list

Portland Sea Dogs

You'll be in Sea Dog heaven with this offer! The Portland Sea Dogs' fan pack is loaded with great stuff: a tattoo of their cool logo, brochure, schedule, and button (depending on availability).

Directions:	Read and follow the instructions on pages 2-8. **Print** your request **neatly** on paper and put it in an envelope. You must enclose a **long self-addressed stamped envelope** and **50¢.**
Write to:	Fan Mail/Souvenir Store Portland Sea Dogs P.O. Box 636 Portland, ME 04104
Ask for:	Logo tattoo, logo button, and souvenir brochure

FREE

FREE

MINOR LEAGUE BASEBALL

Wild Warthogs

The Winston-Salem Warthogs are charging through another year, ferocious as ever. Send for their schedule, souvenir list, and sticker featuring the mascot with an attitude.

Directions:	Read and follow the instructions on pages 2-8. **Print** your request **neatly** on paper and put it in an envelope. You must enclose a **long self-addressed stamped envelope.**
Write to:	Winston-Salem Warthogs Fan Pack P.O. Box 4488 Winston-Salem, NC 27115
Ask for:	Fan pack

Firebird Inferno

Support the Phoenix Firebirds as they leave the rest of the Pacific Coast League in ashes! You'll receive a logo sticker, pocket schedule, souvenir brochure, and information about their Li'l Birds Club.

Directions:	Read and follow the instructions on pages 2-8. **Print** your request **neatly** on paper and put it in an envelope. You must enclose a **long self-addressed stamped envelope.**
Write to:	Phoenix Firebirds Baseball Firebirds Fan Pack P.O. Box 8528 Scottsdale, AZ 85252-8528
Ask for:	Phoenix Firebirds pocket schedule, logo sticker, souvenir brochure, and Li'l Birds Club info

NFL Fan Packs

Show your favorite team what kind of fantastic fan you are by sending for an NFL fan pack. You'll receive *NFL News*, team trivia, and more!
Even if you can't decide on your favorite team, you can ask for the NFL fan pack that covers the entire league.

Directions:	Read and follow the instructions on pages 2-8. **Print** your name, address, and request **neatly** on a postcard.
Write to:	ATTN: Free Stuff for Kids Request Starline Sports Marketing 1480–F Terrell Mill Road, Suite 700 Marietta, GA 30067
Ask for:	NFL fan pack *(specify which team you want)*

Football Fun

The Pro Football Hall of Fame recently opened a new, state-of-the-art rotating theater called GameDay Stadium. This thrilling attraction puts a new spin on your favorite game. Join in the fun with this commemorative milkcap, NFL nickname wordsearch, and brochure.

Directions:	Read and follow the instructions on pages 2-8. **Print** your name, address, and request **neatly** on a postcard. You must also enclose a **long self-addressed stamped envelope.**
Write to:	Pro Football Hall of Fame ATTN: Education Department 2121 George Halas Drive NW Canton, OH 44708
Ask for:	GameDay Stadium milkcap

Chicago Bulls

You can't beat the Chicago Bulls and their winning combo of all-star players. Show the world you're a Bulls fan and send for this fan pack: letter, sticker, schedule, and fan club information.

Directions:	**Read and follow the instructions on pages 2-8. Print** your request **neatly** on paper and put it in an envelope. You must enclose a **long self-addressed stamped envelope.**
Write to:	Chicago Bulls Fan Mail 1901 West Madison Chicago, IL 60612
Ask for:	Chicago Bulls fan pack

BASKETBALL

Piston Power

Catch Detroit Pistons' superstar Grant Hill at the hoop for another season of mind-boggling slam dunks and triple doubles. The fan pack includes a schedule and an 8½-by-11-inch team photo (depending on availability).

Directions:	Read and follow the instructions on pages 2-8. Print your request neatly on paper and put it in an envelope. You must enclose a long self-addressed stamped envelope.
Write to:	Detroit Pistons Two Championship Drive Auburn Hills, MI 48326
Ask for:	Detroit Pistons fan pack

Atlanta Hawks

Get the scoop on who's at the hoop for the Atlanta Hawks this year. Check out the Hawks' hot new logo and send for their bumper sticker and pocket schedule.

Directions:	Read and follow the instructions on pages 2-8. Print your request neatly on paper and put it in an envelope. You must enclose a long self-addressed stamped envelope.
Write to:	Atlanta Hawks ATTN: Fan Mail PR Department One CNN Center, Suite 405 Atlanta, GA 30303
Ask for:	Atlanta Hawks bumper sticker

Capitalize

Make it your goal to get this cool hockey fan pack the Washington Capitals have to offer. You'll receive team history and information letters, and a pocket schedule.

Directions:	**Read and follow the instructions on pages 2-8. Print** your request **neatly** on paper and put it in an envelope. You must enclose a **long self-addressed stamped envelope.**
Write to:	Washington Capitals USAir Arena ATTN: Fan Mail Landover, MD 20785
Ask for:	Team history letter, team info letter, and schedule

Cool and Curling

Do curlers really walk almost two miles during an entire game? Is the game actually played with brooms? Why is curling called "chess on ice"? Find the answers to these questions and more in this informative brochure about the sport that's sweeping the nation.

Directions:	**Read and follow the instructions on pages 2-8. Print** your request **neatly** on paper and put it in an envelope. You must enclose a **long self-addressed stamped envelope.**
Write to:	USA Curling P.O. Box 866 Stevens Point, WI 54481
Ask for:	Curling brochure

Sports Rings

Wear your favorite sport on your finger! Choose from football, basketball, baseball, and soccer and you'll receive a wacky ring perfect for any size finger.

Directions:	Read and follow the instructions on pages 2-8. Print your request neatly on paper and put it in an envelope. You must enclose $1.00.
Write to:	Gift Club Box 1-SR Stony Point, NY 10980
Ask for:	Football ring **or** Basketball ring **or** Baseball ring **or** Soccer ring

Kids on Strike

This offer is going to bowl you over! Crazy characters BIF and BUZZY teach you to bowl in a pamphlet just for kids. And you'll also receive colorful stickers and a bookmark: a bunch of stuff with fun to spare.

ROLL INTO READING...

^BIF is a registered trademark of the YABA. All rights reserved.

BOWLERS RULE!

IN-SCHOOL BOWLING PROGRAM

Directions:	Read and follow the instructions on pages 2-8. Print your request neatly on paper and put it in an envelope. You must enclose a **long self-addressed stamped envelope.**
Write to:	YABA ATTN: BIF & BUZZY–FS 5301 South 76th Street Greendale, WI 53129-1192
Ask for:	BIF–Fundamentals of Bowling pamphlet, sticker, bowling bookmark

MEADOWBROOK PRESS

1997 EDITION

U.S. MAIL

Hobbies and Activities

FREE

Pool Tips

The tips in this pamphlet will show you how to play pool like the pros. You'll learn about the different types of games and how to shoot the ball right. With strategy, skill, and patience, you'll be hitting the pockets in no time.

Directions:	Read and follow the instructions on pages 2-8. Print your request neatly on paper and put it in an envelope. You must enclose a long self-addressed stamped envelope and a 55¢ stamp.
Write to:	BCA 1700 South 1st Avenue Suite 25A Iowa City, IA 52240
Ask for:	How to Play Pool Right booklet

OUTDOOR ACTIVITIES

Canoe with a Clue

Learn how to trek the waters safely. This pamphlet tells beginners all about canoeing and kayaking, from getting the boat into the water to paddling safely through the waves so that *you* don't end up in the water.

Kids in Cars

Did you know that soap box derby racing began with a bunch of kids who made their own cars and held their own races? Find out more about the history of the soap box derby, how a race is run, and how you can be a part of it no matter where you live.

Directions:	Read and follow the instructions on pages 2-8. **Print** your request **neatly** on paper and put it in an envelope. You must enclose a **long self-addressed stamped envelope.**
Write to:	United States Canoe Association P.O. Box 5743 Lafayette, IN 47903
Ask for:	Welcome Paddler! pamphlet

Directions:	Read and follow the instructions on pages 2-8. **Print** your name, address, and request **neatly** on a postcard.
Write to:	All-American Soap Box Derby P.O. Box 7233 Akron, OH 44306
Ask for:	Official All-American Soap Box Derby booklet and price sheet

Footbag Fun

Look, Ma, no hands! Grab your favorite feet and join in the game of footbag—this player's manual will tell you how. In addition, you'll receive information about joining the World Footbag Association and a way-cool sticker for footbag fans.

Directions:	**Read and follow the instructions on pages 2-8. Print** your request **neatly** on paper and put it in an envelope. You must enclose a **long self-addressed stamped envelope.**
Write to:	World Footbag Association 1317 Washington Avenue Suite 7 Golden, CO 80401
Ask for:	Official player's manual and way-cool sticker

Horseshoes and You

Horseshoe pitching has been around for a long time. And there's a reason. Send for this information, including game rules, and find out why it takes more than just luck to send those shoes spinning.

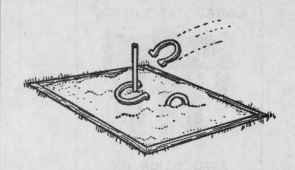

Directions:	**Read and follow the instructions on pages 2-8. Print** your request **neatly** on paper and put it in an envelope. You must enclose a **long self-addressed stamped envelope.**
Write to:	NHPA 10326 Hwy D La Monte, MO 65337
Ask for:	Rules of Horseshoe Pitching pamphlet

Roller Skating Poster

You don't have to be a roller skater to appreciate the colorful and futuristic design of this poster. It features animals skating through space—there's even a cow skating over the moon. Roller skating: It's not just a healthy sport, it's an attitude.

Directions:	Read and follow the instructions on pages 2-8. Print your name, address, and request neatly on paper and put it in an envelope. You must enclose $1.00.
Write to:	Roller Skating Associations 7301 Georgetown Road Suite 123 ATTN: Accounting Indianapolis, IN 46268
Ask for:	Roller Skating poster

Skateboard with a Brain

If you're like most skaters, you're careful about the board you choose to ride (more careful than where you choose to ride it). Send for this free fact sheet about skateboards so you can glide—not collide.

Directions:	Read and follow the instructions on pages 2-8. Print your name, address, and request neatly on a postcard.
Write to:	Publication Request Office of Information and Public Affairs U.S. Consumer Product Safety Commission Washington, DC 20207
Ask for:	#093–Skateboards fact sheet

Play the Harmonica

Learn to play one of the most portable instruments in the world. Harmonica players come in all shapes, sizes, and ages—send for this free Hohner booklet and learn how to become one of them. Within minutes, you will be able to play simple tunes on the harmonica.

Directions:	**Read and follow the instructions on pages 2-8. Print** your request **neatly** on paper and put it in an envelope. You must enclose a **long self-addressed stamped envelope.**
Write to:	Hohner, Inc. P.O. Box 15035 Richmond, VA 23227-0435
Ask for:	How to Play the Hohner Harmonica booklet

Stamp Assortment

You're bound to find stamps you like in this variety pack. You'll receive ten foreign and U.S. stamps, including two stamps of Disney characters. This offer is perfect for collectors and kids with an eye for tiny works of art.

Directions:	**Read and follow the instructions on pages 2-8. Print** your request **neatly** on paper and put it in an envelope. You must enclose a **long self-addressed stamped envelope** and **50¢. Tape coins to cardboard.** *No checks please.*
Write to:	E. Williams P.O. Box 914 Brooklyn, NY 11207-0914
Ask for:	Ten foreign and U.S. stamps

Philat-a-who?

Philatelist. But you don't have to say it to do it. Collecting stamps is a hobby that could last for the rest of your life, and maybe the life of your grandchildren too. Learn more about this timeless hobby.

The Art of Mail

Millions of letters and packages go through the world's mail every day. Millions of stamps, too. Different kinds of stamps reflect different cultures, histories, and heros. Start collecting stamps now and you start collecting the history of life. Send for this newsletter to find out more.

Directions:	Read and follow the instructions on pages 2-8. **Print** your request **neatly** on paper and put it in an envelope. You must enclose a **long self-addressed stamped envelope.**
Write to:	Junior Philatelists of America P.O. Box 850 Boalsburg, PA 16827
Ask for:	Beginning stamp collector's packet

Directions:	Read and follow the instructions on pages 2-8. **Print** your name, address, and request **neatly** on paper and put it in an envelope. You must enclose **$1.00.**
Write to:	Junior Philatelists of America P.O. Box 850 Boalsburg, PA 16827
Ask for:	Beginning stamp collector's newsletter

 FREE

Milkcaps with Attitude

Whether you play the game or just collect the milkcaps, you can't go wrong with the variety and style of this offer. You'll receive five free milkcaps chosen from a whole mess of cool designs, from creepy to cute.

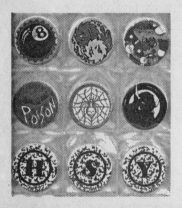

Directions:	Read and follow the instructions on pages 2-8. **Print** your request **neatly** on paper and put it in an envelope. You must enclose a **long self-addressed stamped envelope.**
Write to:	Sunday International 7411 Earl Circle Huntington Beach, CA 92647
Ask for:	Five random milkcaps

Flying Frogs

These are more than just your everyday milkcaps. You can use the small notches in the sides to build shapes like castles, airplanes, and dinosaurs—anything you can think of! And if that isn't enough, use the larger notches to flick them off each other and send them flying. You'll receive eight in one set.

Directions:	Read and follow the instructions on pages 2-8. **Print** your request **neatly** on paper and put it in an envelope. You must enclose a **long self-addressed stamped envelope** and **$1.00.**
Write to:	Scana Enterprises Department FRG P.O. Box 23262 Waco, TX 76702-3262
Ask for:	Flying frogs

Heart Paints

For all you artists out there, this offer is perfect. You get a five-color paint set and brush kept in a heart-shaped case that clicks shut to keep the paint from drying out. Carry this stylish case anywhere you feel like creating a masterpiece.

Directions:	Read and follow the instructions on pages 2-8. Print your name, address, and request neatly on paper and put it in an envelope. You must enclose $1.00.
Write to:	McVehil's Mercantile 45 Bayne Avenue Department HP Washington, PA 15301–8864
Ask for:	Heart paints

Cool and Crafty

Get ready for winter with these craft projects from the north. Make your own penguin basket or candy cane picture frame. Both kits come with materials, instructions, a song with music, and an extra craft for you to try!

Beaded Ring Kit

This kit comes with all the materials (except scissors) you'll need to make three cool beaded rings. Experiment with infinite color and design possibilities. Make them all for yourself or share them with friends.

Directions:	Read and follow the instructions on pages 2-8. Print your name, address, and request neatly on a postcard.
Write to:	Kapers for Kids 1005 10th Avenue SE Minneapolis, MN 55414
Ask for:	Penguin basket kit **or** Candy cane frame kit

Directions:	Read and follow the instructions on pages 2-8. Print your request neatly on paper and put it in an envelope. You must enclose a **long self-addressed stamped envelope** and **$1.00.**
Write to:	Grin 'n' Barrett P.O. Box 1536–B Rialto, CA 92377
Ask for:	Beaded ring kit

Countless Crafts

You're bound to find a craft you love with this huge selection. Choose one of the following Quicksew kits: quickpoint, needlepoint, latchhook, cross-stitch, or crewel embroidery. Or, if that isn't enough to choose from, send for a set of eight craft booklets. Make sure you specify which offer you want.

Directions:	Read and follow the instructions on pages 2-8. Print your name, address, and request neatly on paper and put it in an envelope. You must enclose $1.00.
Write to:	Gift Club Box 1–Q (for Quicksew kit) or Box 1–CB (for craft booklets) Stony Point, NY 10980
Ask for:	One Quicksew kit: quickpoint, needlepoint, latchhook, cross-stitch, or crewel embroidery or eight craft booklets

Teddy Bear Crochet

Crochet away with these instructions for making adorable teddy bear accessories. Choose crochet instructions for either the teddy bear toy bootees or the teddy bear purse. They're unique, fun, and easy to make!

Directions:	Read and follow the instructions on pages 2-8. Print your request neatly on paper and put it in an envelope. You must enclose a long self-addressed stamped envelope.
Write to:	Lorraine Vetter Department TB 7924 Soper Hill Road Everett, WA 98205
Ask for:	Teddy bear purse instructions or Teddy bear bootees instructions

CRAFTS

Project Ideas

Learn ideas for decorating everything from T-shirts, pillows, and sneakers to pennants, bulletin boards, and more. You'll receive a stack of ideas, including instructions, lists of materials, and special bonuses, such as a recipe for making biscuits for your pet.

Directions:	Read and follow the instructions on pages 2-8. Print your request neatly on paper and put it in an envelope. You must enclose a long self-addressed stamped envelope.
Write to:	Delta Technical Coatings, Inc. Department FS 2550 Pellissier Place Whittier, CA 90601-1505
Ask for:	Mom and Me: designs for kids

Flannel Iron-On

Everyone can join the team with these printed flannel iron-ons. All you need is a pullover shirt and an iron—it's easy to be a part of this sporty fashion craze. Choose one of the following stylish options: Varsity, Attitude, University, or Mexico.

Directions:	Read and follow the instructions on pages 2-8. Print your name, address, and request neatly on paper and put it in an envelope. You must enclose $1.00.
Write to:	Pineapple Appeal P.O. Box 197 Owatonna, MN 55060
Ask for:	Printed flannel iron-on

Stencil in Style

Put your name or a short message on everything from school papers to suitcases. Simply choose what your stencil will spell out (up to ten letters and spaces), and you'll receive both the stencil and an activity sheet full of wild and unusual ways you can use your stencil for endless tracing fun.

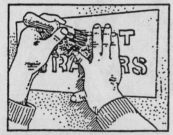

Directions:	Read and follow the instructions on pages 2-8. Print your request neatly on paper and put it in an envelope. You must enclose a long self-addressed stamped envelope and $1.00. Tape coins to cardboard.
Write to:	Great Tracers Department STN 3 Schoenbeck Road Prospect Heights, IL 60070-1435
Ask for:	Stencil (specify name or message up to ten letters and spaces)

Papyrus

The first paper known to humankind, papyrus was originally produced by the ancient Egyptians during the time of the pharaohs, over 4,000 years ago. Made by hand, papyrus can be written on with crayon, ink, acrylic, felt-tipped pen, water colors, gouache, and oil paints. You will receive a 4-by-6-inch craft sheet of blank papyrus and a "Making of Papyrus" information sheet.

Directions:	Read and follow the instructions on pages 2-8. Print your request neatly on paper and put it in an envelope. You must enclose a long self-addressed stamped envelope and $1.00.
Write to:	PAPY-r-US P.O. Box 90128 Santa Barbara, CA 93190-0128
Ask for:	Blank papyrus

Paper Projects

Send away for instructions and materials to make your own decorative frames or 3-D butterflies. The frame kit includes four 4-by-5-inch frames cut from colorful and beautifully designed papers: perfect for framing school pictures! The butterfly comes with paper and patterns.

Directions:	Read and follow the instructions on pages 2-8. Print your name, address, and request **neatly** on paper and put it in an envelope. You must enclose **50¢.**
Write to:	Woolie Works—frame **or** butterfly 6201 East Huffman Road Anchorage, AK 99516
Ask for:	Frame kit **or** Butterfly kit

Origami

The art of paper folding has been around forever. Send for this offer and you'll find out why! You will receive materials and instructions for making either your own decorative bookmark **or** a paper cup that you can actually drink from.

Directions:	Read and follow the instructions on pages 2-8. Print your request **neatly** on paper and put it in an envelope. You must enclose a **long self-addressed stamped envelope** and **50¢. Tape coins to cardboard.** *No checks please.*
Write to:	Phyllis Goodstein Department PC (for paper cup) **or** Department OB (for bookmark) P.O. Box 912 Levittown, NY 11756-0912
Ask for:	Paper cup **or** Origami bookmark

Fun & Games Pad

Ever been bored during a long car ride or while waiting in a doctor's office? This tiny activity pad is full of games to make time fly past while you have a blast. And it's the perfect size to put in your pocket or hold in your hand.

Directions:	Read and follow the instructions on pages 2-8. Print your request neatly on paper and put it in an envelope. You must enclose a long self-addressed stamped envelope and 50¢.
Write to:	Alvin Peters Company Department FGP Empire State Plaza P.O. Box 2400 Albany, NY 12220-0400
Ask for:	Fun & games pad

Lungs That Last

What's more important than even eating and drinking? Breathing! Find out more about your lungs and what smoking does to them. Send for a No Smoking activity book, No Smoking coloring book, and Lungs at Work—No Smoking poster.

Directions:	Read and follow the instructions on pages 2-8. Print your name, address, and request neatly on a postcard.
Write to:	American Lung Association G.P.O. Box 596-75 New York, NY 10116-0596
Ask for:	#0840–No Smoking activity book #0043–No Smoking coloring book #0121–Lungs at Work—No Smoking poster

Toy Safety Coloring Book

What could be more fun to learn about than toys! Grab your crayons and clear a spot on the floor. Each page in this book features tips to help you play safely and a picture for you to color.

Directions:	**Read and follow the instructions on pages 2-8. Print** your name, address, and request **neatly** on a postcard.
Write to:	Publication Request Office of Information and Public Affairs U.S. Consumer Product Safety Commission Washington, DC 20207
Ask for:	#283–Toy Safety coloring book

Pictures and Puzzles

Let Arnold Schwarzenegger teach you about fitness while you color pictures of him and his friends in action. Or, if games are more your style, send for the activity book featuring the Puzzle Squad. Whichever book you choose, you'll have pages of fun at your fingertips.

Directions:	**Read and follow the instructions on pages 2-8. Print** your request **neatly** on paper and put it in an envelope. You must enclose a **9-by-12-inch self-addressed stamped envelope** and **$1.00.**
Write to:	Children's Better Health Institute ATTN: FSFK 97 1100 Waterway Boulevard Indianapolis, IN 46202
Ask for:	Arnold Schwarzenegger's Fitness for Kids coloring book **or** The Best Adventures of the Puzzle Squad activity book

Toys and Fun Stuff

FREE

Goofy Yo-yos

Ever wanted to have the world at your fingertips? Now you can with this global yo-yo. Or, if silly is more your style, choose the hamburger instead— a yummy yo-yo bun that's loads of fun.

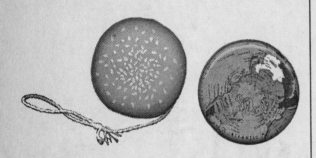

Directions:	Read and follow the instructions on pages 2-8. Print your request neatly on paper and put it in an envelope. You must enclose a long self-addressed stamped envelope and $1.00.
Write to:	Safe Child P.O. Box 40–1594 Brooklyn, NY 11240-1594
Ask for:	Global yo-yo or Hamburger yo-yo

Yo-yo Tricks

From "walking the dog" to going "around the world," this offer will teach you how to make the most of your yo-yo. The tricks are demonstrated by a comic strip that's as fun to read as the stunts are fun to do.

Directions:	Read and follow the instructions on pages 2-8. Print your request neatly on paper and put it in an envelope. You must enclose a long self-addressed stamped envelope.
Write to:	Duncan Toys P.O. Box 97 Middlefield, OH 44062
Ask for:	Yo-yo tricks sheet

Lego® System Blocks

Start a Lego set or add to the set you already have with this mini package of imagination blocks. You'll receive thirteen to sixteen pieces per set to connect into animal shapes, buildings, or whatever you can come up with.

Directions:	Read and follow the instructions on pages 2-8. Print your request neatly on paper and put it in an envelope. You must enclose a long self-addressed stamped envelope with a 55¢ stamp affixed and $1.00.
Write to:	Alvin Peters Company Department LSB Empire State Plaza P.O. Box 2400 Albany, NY 12220-0400
Ask for:	Lego blocks

Pocket Book of Magic

This book is full of tricks that will blow your friends away. Learn some of the oldest secrets in the world and always have something up your sleeve.

Directions:	Read and follow the instructions on pages 2-8. **Print** your request **neatly** on paper and put it in an envelope. You must enclose a **long self-addressed stamped envelope** and **50¢.**
Write to:	Scana Enterprises Department MGC P.O. Box 23262 Waco, TX 76702-3262
Ask for:	Pocket Book of Magic

Abracadabra

These magic tricks are mystifying and simply unbelievable. You can accurately predict a selected card, change $10 of play money into $100, change the color of a card, or make a coin completely disappear! Instructions and props are included. With a little practice, you could be the next Houdini.

Directions:	Read and follow the instructions on pages 2-8. **Print** your request **neatly** on paper and put it in an envelope. You must enclose a **long self-addressed stamped envelope** and **$1.00** for **each trick.** *No checks please.*
Write to:	Phyllis Goodstein Department MT P.O. Box 912 Levittown, NY 11756-0912
Ask for:	Predict a selected card **or** Magic money **or** Color-changing cards **or** Magic coin case

Color-Changing Magic Whistle Flutes

You'll have to see this offer to believe it. These flutes actually change color when you blow into them! You'll receive two flutes in different colors to get you started making musical magic.

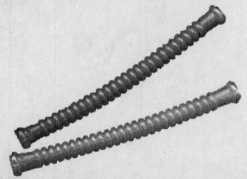

Directions:	Read and follow the instructions on pages 2-8. **Print** your name, address, and request **neatly** on paper and put it in an envelope. You must enclose **$1.00**.
Write to:	NEETSTUF P.O. Box 353 Department FS–32 Rio Grande, NJ 08242
Ask for:	Bobby whistles

Christmas Card Records

You may not want to send these crazy cards to anyone but yourself. They actually contain records that you can play on your turntable. You'll receive three cards with songs that include "Blue Christmas" by Willie Nelson, "Jingle Bells" by the Singing Dogs (dogs actually bark out the song!), and "Deck the Halls" by the Tabbynacle Choir (cats meow this tune).

Directions:	Read and follow the instructions on pages 2-8. **Print** your name, address, and request **neatly** on paper and put it in an envelope. You must enclose **$1.00**.
Write to:	Gift Club Box 11–C Garnerville, NY 10984
Ask for:	Christmas card records

Animals That Grow Before Your Eyes!

This amazing offer features a dinosaur that, when soaked in water, grows to six times its original size, or sea life that grows to two times its original size. Then take them out of the water and watch them shrink.

Directions:	Read and follow the instructions on pages 2-8. Print your request neatly on paper and put it in an envelope. You must enclose a long self-addressed stamped envelope and 80¢.
Write to:	Alvin Peters Company Department SGD (for dinosaur) or Department SGSL (for sea life) Empire State Plaza P.O. Box 2400 Albany, NY 12220-0400
Ask for:	SuperGrow dinosaur or SuperGrow sea life

Bendable Bunny

Even Bugs Bunny can't bend in the ways this kooky toy can. Long and flexible, this bunny will have you in stitches as you tie it in all sorts of nutty knots. The possible positions are endless.

Directions:	Read and follow the instructions on pages 2-8. Print your name, address, and request neatly on paper and put it in an envelope. You must enclose $1.00.
Write to:	McVehil's Mercantile 45 Bayne Avenue Department BB Washington, PA 15301-8864
Ask for:	Bendable bunny

Wire Puzzles

Get ready for some of the hardest puzzles around: wire puzzles. The object is to separate two metal pieces without bending them open. They look easy, but don't be surprised when you spend hours trying to figure them out. You'll receive three puzzles: do them alone or challenge your friends to see who can solve them quicker.

Directions:	Read and follow the instructions on pages 2-8. Print your request neatly on paper and put it in an envelope. You must enclose a long self-addressed stamped envelope and 75¢. Tape coins to paper or cardboard. *No checks please.*
Write to:	Phyllis Goodstein Department WP P.O. Box 912 Levittown, NY 11756-0912
Ask for:	Wire puzzles

Shape-Up Sticks

If you have a steady hand, this is the game for you! The object is to pick up these brightly colored sticks, one by one, without disturbing the other sticks. You receive points for each stick you pick up if you're playing with friends, and the challenge of picking them all up if you're playing alone. You also get a helpful and fun math poem to go along with the game!

Directions:	Read and follow the instructions on pages 2-8. Print your request neatly on paper and put it in an envelope. You must enclose a long self-addressed stamped envelope and $1.00.
Write to:	Reading Realm Department S P.O. Box 274 Barker, TX 77413-0274
Ask for:	Shape-up sticks

Mini-Jet Glider

This Styrofoam glider twists, turns, glides, skims the ground, and loops when thrown into the air. Perfect for tiny hands, this tricky plane can be flown anywhere, indoors and out.

Directions:	Read and follow the instructions on pages 2-8. Print your request neatly on paper and put it in an envelope. You must enclose a long self-addressed stamped envelope and 75¢.
Write to:	Alvin Peters Company Department JG Empire State Plaza P.O. Box 2400 Albany, NY 12220-0400
Ask for:	Mini-jet glider

Amazing Stunt Glider

Made especially for stunts, this large glider will actually fly back to you. The plane comes with stunt directions that take only a little time and patience to master.

Directions:	Read and follow the instructions on pages 2-8. Print your request neatly on paper and put it in an envelope. You must enclose a long self-addressed stamped envelope and $1.00 per glider.
Write to:	Alvin Peters Company Department ASG Empire State Plaza P.O. Box 2400 Albany, NY 12220-0400
Ask for:	Amazing stunt glider

Jump for Joy

Jumping rope is one of the most fun, healthful exercises around. Send away for this jump rope with safety handles and no staples—safe for even the littlest jumper and fun for all.

Directions:	Read and follow the instructions on pages 2-8. Print your name, address, and request neatly on paper and put it in an envelope. You must enclose $1.00.
Write to:	McVehil's Mercantile 45 Bayne Avenue Department JR Washington, PA 15301-8864
Ask for:	Jump rope

Beachball

From beach to playground to stadium, beachballs are a blast. This offer features a full-size beachball with brightly colored stripes. Blow it up and bounce it around by yourself or with friends.

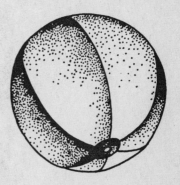

Directions:	Read and follow the instructions on pages 2-8. Print your name, address, and request neatly on paper and put it in an envelope. You must enclose $1.00.
Write to:	McVehil's Mercantile 45 Bayne Avenue Department BL Washington, PA 15301-8864
Ask for:	Beachball

Do Not Disturb!

When you need your privacy, keep brothers, sisters, and parents out with these zany signs. You'll receive two to hang on your doorknob, telling visitors to leave you alone while making them laugh at the funny pictures and messages.

Directions:	Read and follow the instructions on pages 2-8. **Print** your name, address, and request **neatly** on paper and put it in an envelope. You must enclose **$1.00.**
Write to:	Gift Club Box 411-S Thiells, NY 10984
Ask for:	Do Not Disturb signs

Painting on a Pin

Have you ever worn a painting? That sounds silly, but these pins are designed from beautiful, ancient Chinese paintings that include the delicate characters of Chinese writing. You'll receive two of these unique pins to brighten up shirts, jackets, or bookbags.

Directions:	Read and follow the instructions on pages 2-8. Print your name, address, and request neatly on paper and put it in an envelope. You must enclose $1.00.
Write to:	Gift Club Box 11–OP Garnerville, NY 10984
Ask for:	Chinese pin

Recycled Treasures

For this offer, all you have to do is choose your favorite animal or Christmas scene and you'll recieve a pin, magnet, or ornament handmade especially for you! The scenes from recycled Christmas cards are bordered by a hand-crocheted trim. Beautiful and one-of-a-kind.

Directions:	Read and follow the instructions on pages 2-8. Print your request neatly on paper and put it in an envelope. You must enclose a long self-addressed stamped envelope and $1.00.
Write to:	Beverly Scott P.O. Box 55494 Birmingham, AL 35255-5494
Ask for:	Ornament or Pin or Magnet (specify type of scene or animal)

Magnet Madness

Post this magnet on your fridge to remind you and your family to eat right. Choose the "Food Pyramid" magnet in English or Spanish. Large enough so you can't miss them every time you search for a snack.

Directions:	Read and follow the instructions on pages 2-8. Print your name, address, and request **neatly** on paper and put it in an envelope. You must enclose **$1.00.**
Write to:	Pineapple Appeal P.O. Box 197 Owatonna, MN 55060
Ask for:	Food pyramid magnet *(specify English or Spanish)*

Scout Stamp Magnet

Be the envy of your troop with these Boy Scout, Girl Scout, and Smokey Bear stamp magnets. Small enough to stick anywhere, yet big enough to show the world you're a scout without doubt.

Directions:	Read and follow the instructions on pages 2-8. Print your name, address, and request **neatly** on paper and put it in an envelope. You must enclose **$1.00.**
Write to:	Hicks Specialties 1308 68th Lane North Department FS97 Brooklyn Center, MN 55430
Ask for:	Girl Scout stamp magnet **or** Boy Scout stamp magnet **or** Smokey Bear stamp magnet

Paper Doll Postcard

Even if you think you're too old to play with dolls, this vintage look-alike Willimantic Thread postcard is worth collecting. Cut out the clothes and the doll or leave it intact and hang it up, send it to a friend, or just keep it in your postcard collection. This one-of-a-kind card looks like something your parents or grandparents would have had as children.

Directions:	Read and follow the instructions on pages 2-8. **Print** your name, address, and request **neatly** on paper and put it in an envelope. You must enclose **$1.00.**
Write to:	Joan Nyorchuk P.O. Box 47516 Phoenix, AZ 85068-7516
Ask for:	Willimantic Thread postcard

Sticker Postcard

Send it, stick it, or collect it—this unique postcard features six stickers, each with "Drink Coca-Cola" written in a different language, from Arabic to Chinese. Whether you collect stickers, postcards, or Coca-Cola items, you can't go wrong with this triple deal!

Directions:	Read and follow the instructions on pages 2-8. **Print** your name, address, and request **neatly** on a postcard.
Write to:	The Coca-Cola Company Consumer Information Center Department FS P.O. Drawer 1734 Atlanta, GA 30301
Ask for:	Coca-Cola sticker postcard (limit one per request)

Birthday Fun

Millions of things happened on the day you were born. Perhaps nothing as important as your birth, but in this offer you'll find a sampling of interesting tidbits like the prices of things the year you were born (you'll be amazed!), lucky numbers, events that affected the world, and more!

Directions:	Read and follow the instructions on pages 2-8. **Print** your name, address, request, and the month, day, and year of birth **neatly** on paper and put it in an envelope. You must enclose **$1.00**.
Write to:	Fun Fact Greetings 5501 Blank Road Unit A Sebastopol, CA 95472
Ask for:	Birthday fun facts

Go Balloony

These cool heart-shaped balloons are perfect for every balloonatic. Choose a "Happy Birthday" or "I Love You" message balloon or ask for a shiny mylar Garfield or Snoopy balloon. Fun and festive, these balloons are great when you celebrate.

Directions:	Read and follow the instructions on pages 2-8. **Print** your name, address, and request **neatly** on paper and put it in an envelope. You must enclose **$1.00**.
Write to:	MARK-IT P.O. Box 246 Dayton, OH 45405
Ask for:	Happy Birthday balloon **or** I Love You balloon **or** Garfield balloon **or** Snoopy balloon

First Name History

Do you know what your name means? Or what traits and astrological meaning your name has? Answer these questions and more with this complete info sheet about the background of your name.

DAVID

Local origin of name: English
From the Hebrew root name "David"

Meaning: "Beloved', 'friend', or 'darling' 1 Samuel 16:19

Emotional Spectrum • Not confrontational, prefers to accommodate.
Personal Integrity • DAVID, an honest person
Personality • As a people watcher, the world never fails to amaze him.
Relationships • His best friends may not really know him.
Travel & Leisure • While his career is important, his hobby takes front seat!
Career & Money • A career in law would suit DAVID.
Life's Opportunities • The entrepreneur spirit in him is strong.

DAVID's Lucky Numbers: 44 • 36 • 3 • 30 • 32 • 20
DAVID was born under the sign of Aries on March, 22.

Directions:	**Read and follow the instructions on pages 2-8. Print** your request **neatly** on paper and put it in an envelope. You must enclose a **long self-addressed stamped envelope** and **$1.00.**
Write to:	Special Products Department H 34 Romeyn Avenue Amsterdam, NY 12010
Ask for:	First name history

Kinderprint Kit

Put your parents' minds at ease with this child identification kit that includes safety tips, fingerprinting materials, a balloon, and more. Use it for yourself or your younger brother or sister. You're never too young or too old to be safe.

Child Identification Program

Directions:	**Read and follow the instructions on pages 2-8. Print** your request **neatly** on paper and put it in an envelope. You must enclose a **long self-addressed stamped envelope** and **$1.00.**
Write to:	Special Products Department K 34 Romeyn Avenue Amsterdam, NY 12010
Ask for:	Kinderprint kit

Crayon Mirror and Comb Set

No one will believe that the crayon you carry actually contains a mirror and comb hidden inside! This cool and colorful set looks like a giant, flat crayon on the outside while the tools you need to keep your image fresh are on the inside.

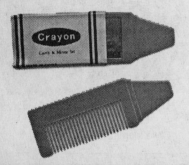

Directions:	Read and follow the instructions on pages 2-8. Print your name, address, and request neatly on paper and put it in an envelope. You must enclose **$1.00.**
Write to:	Mr. Rainbows P.O. Box 908 Department FS–34 Rio Grande, NJ 08242
Ask for:	Crayon mirror and comb set

Fancy Tail

Have fun with your hair, and stay in style. This tool helps you fix your locks in all kinds of cool twists and funky flips. You'll be amazed at how much fun you can have with your hair.

Directions:	Read and follow the instructions on pages 2-8. Print your name, address, and request neatly on paper and put it in an envelope. You must enclose **$1.00.**
Write to:	Gift Club Box 411-FT Thiells, NY 10984
Ask for:	Fancy tail

MEADOWBROOK PRESS

1997 EDITION

U.S. MAIL

Stickers

Barbie™© Scene Stickers

These stickers feature scenes from the lives of Barbie and her friends. It's like having your very own collection of snapshots featuring the classic dolls in action. You'll receive ten stickers.

Directions:	Read and follow the instructions on pages 2-8. Print your request neatly on paper and put it in an envelope. You must enclose a long self-addressed stamped envelope and $1.00.
Write to:	Scana Enterprises Department BBTT P.O. Box 23262 Waco, TX 76702-3262
Ask for:	Barbie stickers

Activity Sticker Sheets

This offer is double the fun! You'll receive stickers and two scenes to place the stickers on. Be creative and make up your own colorful sticker combinations.

Directions:	Read and follow the instructions on pages 2-8. Print your request neatly on paper and put it in an envelope. You must enclose $1.00.
Write to:	Mr. Rainbows P.O. Box 908 Department FS-26 Rio Grande, NJ 08242
Ask for:	Activity sticker sheets

Color-Changing Stickers

Do you have the magic touch? Find out with these stickers that change color when you press on them. You'll receive six stickers of different animal shapes. Put them on your favorite folder and amaze your friends with a touch of your finger.

Directions:	**Read and follow the instructions on pages 2-8. Print** your request **neatly** on paper and put it in an envelope. You must enclose a **long self-addressed stamped envelope** and **75¢.**
Write to:	Smiles 'N' Things P.O. Box 974 Department #2 HS Claremont, CA 91711-0974
Ask for:	Heat-sensitive stickers

TinyToon™© Collectible Stickers

They're tiny, they're toony, they're all a little loony—collect all the hilarious TinyToon characters: Babs and Buster Bunny, Plucky Duck, and more! You'll receive two sets of six stickers—enough to collect and trade with all of your friends.

Directions:	**Read and follow the instructions on pages 2-8. Print** your request **neatly** on paper and put it in an envelope. You must enclose a **long self-addressed stamped envelope** and **75¢.**
Write to:	Alvin Peters Company Department TTCS Empire State Plaza P.O. Box 2400 Albany, NY 12220-0400
Ask for:	TinyToon collectible stickers

Animaniacs™© or Tiny-Toon™© Prism Stickers

These stickers feature the funniest cartoon characters on TV and they also shine like rainbows in the light. Choose either Animaniacs or TinyToon stickers—both are guaranteed to make you chuckle.

Directions:	**Read and follow the instructions on pages 2-8. Print** your request **neatly** on paper and put it in an envelope. You must enclose a **long self-addressed stamped envelope** and **80¢** for **each set** of stickers.
Write to:	Alvin Peters Company Department TTPS (for TinyToon) **or** APS (for Animaniacs) Empire State Plaza P.O. Box 2400 Albany, NY 12220-0400
Ask for:	TinyToon prism stickers **or** Animaniacs prism stickers

Happy Face Prism Stickers

Want to cheer up a friend who's down? Surprise him or her with these happy face prism stickers that sparkle in the light with the colors of the rainbow. You'll receive thirty stickers—plenty to give to friends and still have enough left over to bring a smile to your own face.

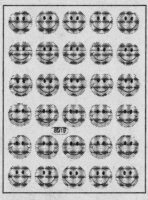

Directions:	**Read and follow the instructions on pages 2-8. Print** your request **neatly** on paper and put it in an envelope. You must enclose a **long self-addressed stamped envelope** and **$1.00.**
Write to:	Stickers 'N' Stuff, Inc. Department Happy P.O. Box 430 Louisville, CO 80027-0430
Ask for:	Happy face stickers

Dinosaur Hologram Stickers

The prehistoric age meets the space age with these wacky stickers: Each one includes the name of the dinosaur as well as an awesome image that actually appears to move! You'll receive twelve stickers— keep them all or trade them with friends.

Directions:	Read and follow the instructions on pages 2-8. Print your request neatly on paper and put it in an envelope. You must enclose a long self-addressed stamped envelope and $1.00.
Write to:	Stickers 'N' Stuff, Inc. Department MH-D P.O. Box 430 Louisville, CO 80027-0430
Ask for:	Dinosaur hologram stickers

African Wildlife Stickers

Take a walk on the wild side with these eye-catching stickers! They feature lions, giraffes, gorillas, zebras, elephants, and other African critters. You'll receive eight different animals on 1½-inch round stickers.

Directions:	Read and follow the instructions on pages 2-8. Print your request neatly on paper and put it in an envelope. You must enclose a long self-addressed stamped envelope and 50¢. Tape coins to cardboard. No checks please.
Write to:	Phyllis Goodstein Department AWS P.O. Box 912 Levittown, NY 11756-0912
Ask for:	African wildlife stickers

Fuzzy Animal Stickers

Enjoy the virtual reality of these stickers: They look and feel like real animals! Soft, fuzzy, and adorable, they are perfect for animal lovers. Choose two squares of stickers from the following: penguins, pandas, cats and mice, cows, horses, guinea pigs, dogs and bones, koalas, and raccoons.

Directions:	Read and follow the instructions on pages 2-8. Print your request neatly on paper and put it in an envelope. You must enclose **$1.00.**
Write to:	Mr. Rainbows P.O. Box 908 Department 27 Rio Grande, NJ 08242
Ask for:	Two squares of fuzzy animal stickers (specify which **two** kinds of animals you want)

Dog Stickers

Anyone with a soft spot for dogs will be howling over these stickers. "Cute" and "cuddly" are the only words to describe them. You'll receive four different, 1½-inch, round stickers.

Directions:	Read and follow the instructions on pages 2-8. Print your request neatly on paper and put it in an envelope. You must enclose a **long self-addressed stamped envelope** and **50¢. Tape coins to cardboard.** No checks please.
Write to:	Phyllis Goodstein Department DGS P.O. Box 912 Levittown, NY 11756-0912
Ask for:	Dog stickers

The World on a Sticker

This set of four stickers is like owning your own globe. Each sticker portrays a different region of Earth. Together, they form a map of the world. Can you name the areas and countries on each sticker? Move over Carmen Sandiego!

Directions:	Read and follow the instructions on pages 2-8. **Print** your request **neatly** on paper and put it in an envelope. You must enclose a **long self-addressed stamped envelope** and **50¢. Tape coins to cardboard.** *No checks please.*
Write to:	Phyllis Goodstein Department ES P.O. Box 912 Levittown, NY 11756-0912
Ask for:	Rotating Earth stickers

Stickers by the Bunch

Cool snowmen or warm hearts—you won't be disappointed with either choice because you'll receive a sheet of *one hundred* stickers! Put them on envelopes or even sign letters with them instead of your name.

Directions:	Read and follow the instructions on pages 2-8. **Print** your request **neatly** on paper and put it in an envelope. You must enclose a **long self-addressed stamped envelope** and **$1.00.**
Write to:	The Very Best P.O. Box 2838 Department M97 Long Beach, CA 90801-2838
Ask for:	Heart stickers **or** Snowmen stickers

LuvNut Stickers

Let the world know what you are nuts over with these LuvNut stickers featuring your favorite sport or hobby: baseball, football, hockey, basketball, fishing, scuba diving, soccer, photography, volleyball, skating, surfing, biking, computers, or just sports in general.

Directions:	Read and follow the instructions on pages 2-8. **Print** your request **neatly** on paper and put it in an envelope. You must enclose a **long self-addressed stamped envelope** and **50¢.**
Write to:	Luvable Characters 2106 Hoffnagle Street Sports 'N' Novelty Department Philadelphia, PA 19152
Ask for:	LuvNut sticker (*choose one from the sports and hobbies listed above*)

Funny Purple Dinosaur Tattoos

Have you ever seen Barney skateboarding? Boxing? Riding a motorcycle and sporting some sweet shades? Of course not! Get ready for a purple dinosaur with an attitude. You'll receive six different tattoos chosen at random.

Directions:	**Read and follow the instructions on pages 2-8. Print** your request **neatly** on paper and put it in an envelope. You must enclose a **long self-addressed stamped envelope** and **75¢**.
Write to:	Alvin Peters Company Department PDT Empire State Plaza P.O. Box 2400 Albany, NY 12220-0400
Ask for:	Funny purple dino tattoos

Assorted Tattoos

Here's an offer your parents are going to love! Simply apply a tattoo to your arm or leg and wait until you see the looks on their faces before telling them it's only temporary. Let these tattoos take you from tiny to tough.

Directions:	**Read and follow the instructions on pages 2-8. Print** your request **neatly** on paper and put it in an envelope. You must enclose **$1.00**.
Write to:	McVehil's Mercantile 45 Bayne Avenue Department TA Washington, PA 15301-8864
Ask for:	Tattoo assortment

MEADOWBROOK PRESS

1997
EDITION

U.S.
MAIL

School Supplies

Puzzle Eraser

If you want a challenge, try this puzzler. You'll receive six colorful interlocking pieces that you put together to form a cube. It's not as easy as it looks, but don't worry if you can't figure it out because each piece is also a handy eraser. A great mind game.

Directions:	Read and follow the instructions on pages 2-8. Print your request neatly on paper and put it in an envelope. You must enclose a long self-addressed stamped envelope and $1.00. Tape coins to cardboard. No checks please.
Write to:	Phyllis Goodstein Department PE P.O. Box 912 Levittown, NY 11756-0912
Ask for:	Puzzle eraser

Bunny Eraser Set

These erasers are so cute you won't want to use them. They come in a set that includes a large bunny in coveralls, a tiny basket, and a chickadee. Use them for school or start a collection.

Directions:	Read and follow the instructions on pages 2-8. Print your request neatly on paper and put it in an envelope. You must enclose $1.00.
Write to:	Smiles 'N' Things P.O. Box 974 Department #3 BE Claremont, CA 91711-0974
Ask for:	Bunny eraser set

Clown Pen

Clown around in class with this clown pen necklace that is certain to attract attention. Simply wear it around your neck and you'll never be without a pen again.

Flags-of-All-Nations Pencil

This colorful and attractive pencil features pictures of flags from countries all around the world. You will receive a 6-inch pencil that never needs sharpening and eleven refill leads. Each pencil comes with a cap and eraser too.

Directions:	Read and follow the instructions on pages 2-8. **Print** your request **neatly** on paper and put it in an envelope. You must enclose a **long self-addressed stamped envelope** and **$1.00**.
Write to:	The Complete Collegiate 490 Route 46 East Department FS Fairfield, NJ 07004
Ask for:	Clown pen necklace

Directions:	Read and follow the instructions on pages 2-8. **Print** your request **neatly** on paper and put it in an envelope. You must enclose a **long self-addressed stamped envelope** and **75¢. Tape coins to cardboard.** *No checks please.*
Write to:	Phyllis Goodstein Department FPC P.O. Box 912 Levittown, NY 11756-0912
Ask for:	Flags-of-all-nations pencil

Magic Wand Pencils

Not only do these silver pencils shimmer and shine, they also come with glittery removable tops: your choice of either a star or a heart. Use your magic wand pencils to make your homework so fun it seems to disappear!

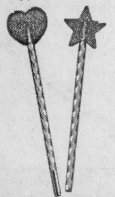

Directions:	**Read and follow the instructions on pages 2-8. Print** your request **neatly** on paper and put it in an envelope. You must enclose **$1.00.**
Write to:	Smiles 'N' Things P.O. Box 974 Department #1 SP (for star pencil) or #2 HP (for heart pencil) Claremont, CA 91711-0974
Ask for:	Star pencil **or** Heart pencil

Fruit-Scented Pencils

These fruity pencils will let your nose do the sniffing while your fingers do the writing. Each pencil comes with eleven refill leads. Choose lemon, strawberry, cherry, grape, or orange.

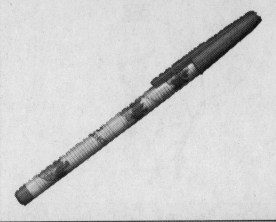

Directions:	**Read and follow the instructions on pages 2-8. Print** your request **neatly** on paper and put it in an envelope. You must enclose a **long self-addressed stamped envelope** and **50¢.**
Write to:	Anita Jones 3808 Bch Ch Drive #11B Far Rockaway, NY 11691-1438
Ask for:	Fruity pencil (*specify which fruit*)

Sign Language Pencil & Postcard

Did you know that the number of hearing-impaired people in the United States is nearly equal to the entire population of Canada? Imagine, then, how many of the people you see every day use sign language to communicate. Now you can learn to fingerspell the letters of the alphabet with this pencil and postcard. Learn to say anything to friends and family without ever making a sound!

Directions:	Read and follow the instructions on pages 2-8. **Print** your request **neatly** on paper and put it in an envelope. You must enclose a **long self-addressed stamped envelope** and **$1.00.**
Write to:	Keep Quiet Box 367 Stanhope, NJ 07874
Ask for:	Sign language pencil and postcard

Stencil-Comb-Ruler

Now you can trace a picture, measure almost anything, and keep every hair in place with one terrific tool. This combination stencil-comb-ruler is handy in class and between classes. You'll never go anywhere without it.

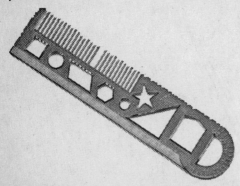

Directions:	Read and follow the instructions on pages 2-8. Print your request neatly on paper and put it in an envelope. You must enclose a long self-addressed stamped envelope and $1.00.
Write to:	The Complete Collegiate 490 Route 46 East Department FS Fairfield, NJ 07004
Ask for:	Stencil-comb-ruler

Wrist Pouch

Keep coins, erasers, milkcaps, or even notes from your friends in this colorful wrist pouch. It comes in neon colors and fastens to your wrist with Velcro so it's easy to put on and take off, leaving your hands free for more important things. You'll never lose your lunch money again!

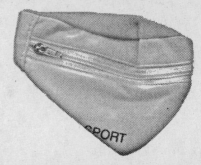

Directions:	Read and follow the instructions on pages 2-8. Print your request neatly on paper and put it in an envelope. You must enclose a long self-addressed stamped envelope and $1.00.
Write to:	The Complete Collegiate 490 Route 46 East Department FS Fairfield, NJ 07004
Ask for:	Wrist pouch

Paperclips

You can never have too many paperclips, especially when they come in shapes, sizes, and colors like these. You'll want to hold onto these colorful clips, and you'll be able to because they come in a clear pouch, keeping even the tiniest clip from getting lost.

Directions:	Read and follow the instructions on pages 2-8. **Print** your request **neatly** on paper and put it in an envelope. You must enclose a **long self-addressed stamped envelope.**
Write to:	Baumgarten's 144 Ottley Drive NE Atlanta, GA 30324
Ask for:	Paperclips

Hobby and Animal Stamps

Stamp an impression of who you are with these rubber stamps featuring your favorite hobby and animal. You will receive two stamps with easy instructions.

Directions:	**Read and follow the instructions on pages 2-8. Print** your request **neatly** on paper and put it in an envelope. You must enclose a **long self-addressed stamped envelope** and **two first-class stamps.** Enclose an additional **first-class stamp** for **each** rubber stamp you request over two.
Write to:	RAMASTAMPS-RS 7924 Soper Hill Road Everett, WA 98205
Ask for:	Two hobby stamps (*specify your favorites*) **or** Two animal stamps (*specify your favorites*) **or** One animal/one hobby stamp (*specify your favorites*)

Name Stamp

Stamp your name on homework, notes, folders, and more. This rubber stamp comes with a wooden handle and any name you choose (up to ten letters).

Directions:	**Read and follow the instructions on pages 2-8. Print** your request **neatly** on paper and put it in an envelope. You must enclose **$1.00.** *No coins please.*
Write to:	RAMASTAMPS-FN 7924 Soper Hill Road Everett, WA 98205
Ask for:	First name stamp (*print the name of your choice clearly*)

Reading

Stash Your Trash

Everybody hates litter, but not everyone knows how to stop the litter problem. Write for these pamphlets, each of which is filled with tips on how you can make America more beautiful and keep it that way.

Directions:	Read and follow the instructions on pages 2-8. **Print** your request **neatly** on paper and put it in an envelope. You must enclose a **long self-addressed stamped envelope.**
Write to:	Keep America Beautiful 1010 Washington Blvd. Stanford, CT 06901
Ask for:	Tips for Preventing Litter, Take Care of America, and Woody's Wise Waste Handling Tips

KIND Kids

Find out how you can be a KIND (Kids in Nature's Defense) kid who cares about the environment and all the creatures who share it. This newspaper created just for kids contains colorful photos, games, puzzles, fun facts, and interviews with famous people—even famous kids! Specify your grade level to make sure you get the issue designed with kids like you in mind.

Directions:	Read and follow the instructions on pages 2-8. **Print** your request **neatly** on paper and put it in an envelope. You must enclose a **long self-addressed stamped envelope.**
Write to:	KIND News Department FSK P.O. Box 362 East Haddam, CT 06423-0362
Ask for:	KIND News Primary (grades K–2) **or** KIND News Junior (grades 3 & 4) **or** KIND News Senior (grades 5 & 6)

FREE

Read about Stuttering

Did you know that Marilyn Monroe was a stutterer? So is actor James Earl Jones, Bob Love of the Chicago Bulls, and many more successful people who have learned from their stuttering problem and gone on to do great things with their lives. If you stutter or know someone who stutters, write for this free information.

STUTTERING
FOUNDATION
OF AMERICA

Directions:	**Read and follow the instructions on pages 2-8. Print** your name, address, and request **neatly** on a postcard.
Write to:	Stuttering Foundation P.O. Box 11749 Memphis, TN 38111-0749
Ask for:	Brochures and fact sheet

GENERAL INTEREST

Learn about Modeling

Train to be a model...or just look like one! Send for Barbizon's booklet and newsletter to learn all about the modeling profession and how you can develop your poise and confidence.

Directions:	Read and follow the instructions on pages 2-8. Print your name, address, and request neatly on a postcard.
Write to:	Barbizon Information Center Department FK 2240 Woolbright Road, #300 Boynton Beach, FL 33426
Ask for:	Modeling newsletter and booklet

Sink Your Teeth into This!

Where would you be without your teeth? They bite, chop, grind, squash, mash, chew, and, of course, smile. Write for these teeth tips to make sure your little white buddies are alive and biting as long as you are.

Directions:	Read and follow the instructions on pages 2-8. Print your request neatly on paper and put it in an envelope. You must enclose a long self-addressed stamped envelope.
Write to:	Johnson & Johnson CPI/Info Center 199 Grandview Road Department: TIPS Skillman, NJ 08558-9418
Ask for:	Tips on Flossing brochure or Tips on Brushing brochure or Tips on Rinsing brochure or Tips on Interdental Cleaning brochure or Ask for more than one

Money Funnies

What if we all carried fish in our wallets instead of dollar bills? What if every state had its own dollar? Why is saving your money important? Find the answers to these questions and more in these funny comics about everything from foreign trade to saving your allowance.

Directions:	Read and follow the instructions on pages 2-8. Print your name, address, and request neatly on a postcard.
Write to:	Federal Reserve Bank of New York Public Information Department 33 Liberty Street, 13th Floor New York, NY 10445
Ask for:	Story of Money comic book or Story of Banks comic book or Once Upon a Dime comic book or A Penny Saved . . . comic book or Story of Foreign Trade comic book

Sprocketman Comic

Strap on your helmet, turn on your bike light, and get ready for a ride with Sprocketman! Follow the adventures of this bicycle hero as he shows you what pedal power is all about—using your brain when you ride.

Directions:	Read and follow the instructions on pages 2-8. Print your name, address, and request neatly on a postcard.
Write to:	Publication Request Office of Information and Public Affairs U.S. Consumer Product Safety Commission Washington, DC 20207
Ask for:	#341-Sprocketman comic book

Reader's Paradise

Do you like puzzles, hidden pictures, dot-to-dots, coloring pages, poems, stories, games, recipes, cartoons, jokes, comics, articles, book reviews, fun facts, works by other kids, or activities? Yes? Then you've stopped at the right page. These incredible magazines offer all this and more for kids of every age group.

Directions:	Read and follow the instructions on pages 2-8. Print your name, address, and request neatly on paper and put it in an envelope. You must enclose $1.00 for each magazine you request. (Issues mailed will be back copies.)
Write to:	Children's Better Health Institute ATTN: FSFK97 1100 Waterway Boulevard Indianapolis, IN 46202
Ask for:	Turtle magazine (ages 2–5) or Humpty Dumpty's magazine (ages 4–6) or Children's Playmate magazine (ages 6–8) or Jack and Jill magazine (ages 7–10) or Child Life magazine (ages 9–11) or Children's Digest magazine (preteen)

Skipping Stones

Skipping Stones is a nonprofit children's magazine that provides a playful forum for sharing ideas and experiences with children from different lands and backgrounds. Learn about kids from all over the globe through their writing, artwork, photos, and more. Make a new friend through the Pen Pals Wanted Pages or simply let your mind travel the world.

Share Your Ideas with the World

Skipping Stones, an award-winning multicultural magazine for children, is looking for your creative thoughts and ideas. They accept art and original writings in every language and from all ages. Don't pass this up: What you have to share is important! You have nothing to lose and the world to gain.

Directions:	**Read and follow the instructions on pages 2-8. Print** your request **neatly** on paper and put it in an envelope. You must enclose **4 stamps** with a **long self-addressed 9-by-12-inch envelope** and **$1.00.**
Write to:	Skipping Stones Magazine P.O. Box 3939 Department FSK97 Eugene, OR 97403-0939
Ask for:	Skipping Stones magazine

Directions:	**Read and follow the instructions on pages 2-8. Print** your request **neatly** on paper and put it in an envelope. You must enclose a **long self-addressed stamped envelope.**
Write to:	Skipping Stones Magazine P.O. Box 3939 Department FSK97 Eugene, OR 97403-0939
Ask for:	Skipping Stones guidelines and brochure

The Pear Bear Chronicles

Follow the adventures of Pear Bear and his animal friends as they sing, dance, and celebrate being healthy and alive. This storybook contains beautiful illustrations, fun facts, and even a coloring page at the end.

Directions:	Read and follow the instructions on pages 2-8. **Print** your request **neatly** on paper and put it in an envelope. You must enclose a **long self-addressed stamped envelope** and **75¢.**
Write to:	ATTN: Studio Kids Oregon, Washington, California Pear Bureau 813 SW Alder Portland, OR 97205-3182
Ask for:	Pear Bear Chronicles

Pear Bear Poster

Make room on your wall for this poster because it is over 2 ½ feet long! The poster features a colorful illustration of Pear Bear and his friends in a lively, magical forest scene with information about pears and your health at the bottom.

Directions:	Read and follow the instructions on pages 2-8. **Print** your request **neatly** on paper and put it in an envelope. You must enclose a **long self-addressed stamped envelope** and **75¢.**
Write to:	ATTN: Studio Kids Oregon, Washington, California Pear Bureau 813 SW Alder Portland, OR 97205-3182
Ask for:	Pear Bear poster

Girls with Guts

Welcome to a world where girls are the heroes—our world! Isn't it about time we saw the stories of courageous and clever female characters? The *Girls to the Rescue* series features tales of daring girls from all over the globe. You'll receive a bookmark *and* sticker to show everyone that you know the true meaning of girl power.

Directions:	**Read and follow the instructions on pages 2-8. Print** your request **neatly** on paper and put it in an envelope. You must enclose a **long self-addressed stamped envelope** and **25¢.**
Write to:	Meadowbrook Press ATTN: GTR 18318 Minnetonka Boulevard Deephaven, MN 55391
Ask for:	Girls to the Rescue bookmark and sticker

Cartoon Bookmark

Now the looniest cartoon characters on TV are here to save your spot in your favorite books. Choose a TinyToon™© or Animaniacs™© bookmark and use it to mark the coolest *Free Stuff* offers.

Directions:	Read and follow the instructions on pages 2-8. Print your request neatly on paper and put it in an envelope. You must enclose a long self-addressed stamped envelope and 50¢.
Write to:	Anita Jones/FSB 3808 BCH CH Drive #11B Far Rockaway, NY 11691-1438
Ask for:	TinyToon bookmark **or** Animaniacs bookmark

Poetry Party!

If you like to chuckle, giggle, snicker, and grin, get ready for the poet kids and teachers call the "King of Giggle Poetry." *Bruce Lansky's Poetry Party* is a book of kid-tested poems guaranteed to make you laugh. Send away for this bookmark that contains a sample of poems from the book and you'll receive a surprise bookmark too!

Directions:	Read and follow the instructions on pages 2-8. Print your request neatly on paper and put it in an envelope. You must enclose a long self-addressed stamped envelope.
Write to:	Meadowbrook Press Department BLPP 18318 Minnetonka Boulevard Deephaven, MN 55391
Ask for:	Poetry Party bookmark

MEADOWBROOK PRESS

1997
EDITION

U.S.
MAIL

Animals

ANIMAL RIGHTS

Kids' Best Friends

If you love animals of all kinds—from dogs to tarantulas—you can't pass up this offer. Even if you don't love animals, you will after reading this magazine filled with stories about amazing animals and the equally amazing people who love them, kids and adults alike. And if that isn't enough, you'll also receive the pamphlet "Careers Helping Animals," with information about how to turn your love of the world's creatures into a way of life.

Directions:	Read and follow the instructions on pages 2-8. Print your name, address, and request neatly on paper and put it in an envelope or use a postcard.
Write to:	Nathania Gartman Box 13 Kanab, UT 84741
Ask for:	Best Friends magazine and Career Helping Animals pamphlet

Learn to Say No

Maybe you've heard stories about people dissecting animals in science classes. Maybe you've been told to do it in your own school and you didn't know that you had a choice: you do. Write for this free booklet that explains why dissection isn't necessary and how you can say no to dissecting animals in school.

Directions:	Read and follow the instructions on pages 2-8. Print your name, address, and request neatly on paper and put it in an envelope or use a postcard.
Write to:	National Anti-Vivisection Society Dissection Hotline 53 West Jackson Boulevard Suite 1552 Chicago, IL 60604
Ask for:	Saying No to Dissection (grades K-6)

Farm Fun

You can tell these offers are fun by the names: Pig Puzzler, Holy Cow!, and Cock-a-Doodle-Do-It. Choose the animal you're interested in learning about, and you'll receive activities that tell you more about it.

Directions:	Read and follow the instructions on pages 2-8. Print your request neatly on paper and put it in an envelope. You must enclose a long self-addressed stamped envelope for each activity you choose.
Write to:	Animal Place 3448 Laguna Creek Trail Vacaville, CA 95688
Ask for:	Pig Puzzler or Holy Cow! or Cock-a-Doodle-Do-It

Horse Charm

This offer includes a gajillion resources to help you find out everything you've ever wanted to know about breeds of horses, where to go to a horse school, horse clubs, and more! You'll also receive a horse charm.

Directions:	Read and follow the instructions on pages 2-8. Print your request on paper and put it in an envelope. You must enclose a long self-addressed stamped envelope and $1.00.
Write to:	Horse Source Department FS 637 Meadows Drive Wenatchee, WA 98801
Ask for:	Horse charm and horse breed directory or Horse club directory or Horse school directory

Horse Sense

Would you like to go horseback riding? Make your ride safer and more fun by sending for these tips from the riding experts on how to find the best stable in your area. Pamphlet includes valuable suggestions on what to look for in riding stables, programs, lessons, and trail riding.

Directions:	Read and follow the instructions on pages 2-8. Print your name, address, and request neatly on a postcard.
Write to:	American Horse Shows Association, Inc. 220 East 42nd Street New York, NY 10017-5876
Ask for:	A Smart Start to Riding brochure

Arabian Horses

If you love Arabian horses, send away for this free informational packet and learn more about them. You can also request essay and photography contest guidelines and find out how you can share your thoughts and pictures with others who share your interests.

Directions:	Read and follow the instructions on pages 2-8. Print your name, address, and request neatly on a postcard.
Write to:	International Arabian Horse Association 10805 East Bethany Drive Aurora, CO 80014
Ask for:	IAHA general information packet and youth essay contest and Arabian horse photography contest entry forms

A Tail from Outer Space

What would you do if we kept people in cages until, if no one wanted them, we killed them? Sounds horrible, doesn't it? Yet that is exactly what happens to animals all over the world. This comic puts people in their pets' shoes (or paws) through the story of a far-off planet where animals rule the world and humans are pets.

Directions:	Read and follow the instructions on pages 2-8. Print your request neatly on paper and put it in an envelope. You must enclose a long self-addressed stamped envelope.
Write to:	The Fund for Animals 808 Alamo Drive Suite 306 Vacaville, CA 95688
Ask for:	A Tail from Outer Space

Pet Sticker

This sticker shows the world that you stick by your pet. You'll also receive a brochure that tells you how veterinarians keep your favorite critter healthy and what you need to know to help them.

Directions:	Read and follow the instructions on pages 2-8. Print your request neatly on paper and put it in an envelope. You must enclose a long self-addressed stamped envelope.
Write to:	American Animal Hospital Association MSC P.O. Box 150899 Denver, CO 80228
Ask for:	Health exam brochure and caring kids sticker

 FREE

Doggie Dreams

What happens to dogs who are left at animal shelters? Do they find a home? Do they live there forever? Or worse? In this book, you not only read about what happens to a dog and her puppies when they're left at a shelter, you get to decide how the story ends.

Directions:	**Read and follow the instructions on pages 2-8. Print** your request **neatly** on paper and put it in an envelope. You must enclose a **long self-addressed stamped envelope.**
Write to:	The Fund for Animals 808 Alamo Drive Suite 306 Vacaville, CA 95688
Ask for:	Dog coloring storybook *(grades K-2; specify Spanish or English)* **or** Dog storybook *(grades 3-5; specify Spanish or English)*

Stamp Magnet

These magnets are collector's items for cat and dog lovers. They'll stick to your fridge, the inside of your locker, or any other metal surface. And they're not just ordinary magnets, either—they're real postage stamps coated so they'll last forever (unless your cat or dog gets ahold of them!).

Directions:	**Read and follow the instructions on pages 2-8. Print** your request **neatly** on paper and put it in an envelope. You must enclose **$1.00.**
Write to:	Hicks Specialties 1308 68th Lane North Department FS97 Brooklyn Center, MN 55430
Ask for:	Cat stamp magnet **or** Dog stamp magnet

Gorilla Poster

Maybe the only gorilla you know by name is your older brother, but that will change when you send for this poster of Koko the Gorilla hanging out with her favorite feline. You'll also receive information about gorillas written just for kids!

Directions:	Read and follow the instructions on pages 2-8. Print your name, address, and request neatly on a postcard.
Write to:	The Gorilla Foundation WFSK Box 620-530 Woodside, CA 94062
Ask for:	Koko the Gorilla poster and kids' info packet

Beaver Fever

What if you had to build your own house on water using your teeth, hands, and tail? What if you had such unexpected neighbors as swallows, snakes, mice, and muskrats sharing your home? No wonder they call the beaver's home a lodge! Find out more about this incredible animal. You'll receive an article about beavers and two coloring sheets too.

Directions:	Read and follow the instructions on pages 2-8. Print your request neatly on paper and put it in an envelope. You must enclose a long self-addressed stamped envelope or the materials will not be sent.
Write to:	Unexpected Wildlife Refuge P.O. Box 765 Department M Newfield, NJ 08344
Ask for:	Beaver coloring sheets and info

 FREE

Wonders of the Wild

Would you believe a Komodo dragon smells in stereo? With its tongue? Do gorillas really build nests? Does a white tiger have icy-blue eyes? Find the answers to these questions and more in these fact-filled pamphlets from the Cincinnati Zoo. Choose which animal you want to learn about.

Directions:	Read and follow the instructions on pages 2-8. **Print** your request **neatly** on paper and put it in an envelope. You must enclose a **long self-addressed stamped envelope** for each pamphlet request.
Write to:	Cincinnati Zoo P.O. Box 198073 School Services Education Department Cincinnati, OH 45219-8073
Ask for:	Bengal Tigers pamphlet **or** Komodo Dragons pamphlet **or** Gorillas pamphlet

Frog Finger Puppets

This offer is perfect for either the beginning frog collector or the avid frog fan. You'll receive the booklet "How to Begin Collecting Frogs," with frog facts and more. On top of that, you'll receive two frog finger puppets. Make your frogs do goofy things like dance, kickbox, or tiptoe. Frog fun for everyone!

Directions:	Read and follow the instructions on pages 2-8. **Print** your request **neatly** on paper and put it in an envelope. You must enclose **$1.00.**
Write to:	The Frog Pond Department K97 P.O. Box 193 Beech Grove, IN 46107
Ask for:	Frog finger puppets and booklet

MEADOWBROOK PRESS
1997 EDITION

U.S. MAIL

U.S. History
and Culture

Gettysburg Booklet

Find out about the historic site of Gettysburg with this 64-page booklet that describes the town, its history, and its significance to all Americans. The booklet even includes a copy of Lincoln's famous Gettysburg Address.

Directions:	Read and follow the instructions on pages 2-8. **Print** your request **neatly** on paper and put it in an envelope. You must enclose a **6 ½-by-9 ½-inch self-addressed stamped envelope.**
Write to:	Gettysburg CVB Department 701 35 Carlisle Street Gettysburg, PA 17325-1899
Ask for:	Gettysburg booklet

Historical Parchments

How would you like your own copy of the Declaration of Independence, the Constitution, or a document filled with photos of all the presidents through Bill Clinton, complete with their signatures? Choose any one of the above three, and you will receive a parchment that looks and feels like it is hundreds of years old.

Directions:	Read and follow the instructions on pages 2-8. **Print** your name, address, and request **neatly** on paper and put it in an envelope. You must enclose a **long self-addressed stamped envelope** and **$1.00.**
Write to:	Mr. Rainbows P.O. Box 908 Department FS–25 Rio Grande, NJ 08242
Ask for:	Declaration of Independence **or** The Constitution **or** Presidential parchment

Patriotic Stencils

Trace a face or place from the past or present. Choose four stencils from the following list of U.S. leaders and symbols: Lincoln, Washington, the flag, the Capitol, the White House, or the Statue of Liberty. Amaze your friends with flawless drawings of familiar buildings and people.

Directions:	Read and follow the instructions on pages 2-8. **Print** your request **neatly** on paper and put it in an envelope. You must enclose a **long self-addressed stamped envelope** and **50¢**.
Write to:	Fax Marketing 460 Carrollton Drive Department 97 Frederick, MD 21701
Ask for:	Patriotic stencils

Presidential Ruler

Did you know that the first U.S. flag had a snake on it? Do you know who our tenth president was? How about the words to the "Star Spangled Banner"? Find out all this and more with this ruler that shows pictures of all the presidents from Washington to Clinton, the evolution of flag design, and the words to the "Star Spangled Banner." You won't find a cooler ruler anywhere.

Directions:	Read and follow the instructions on pages 2-8. **Print** your name, address, and request **neatly** on paper and put it in an envelope. You must enclose **$1.00**.
Write to:	Smiles 'N' Things P.O. Box 974 Department #3–PFR Claremont, CA 91711-0974
Ask for:	Presidential ruler

Flag Keychains

"Oh say can you see that a flag holds your key?" These solid keychains hang from a United States flag for you to jiggle and wave every time you unlock a door. You'll receive two keychains so you can keep one for yourself and give one to a friend.

Directions:	Read and follow the instructions on pages 2-8. Print your request neatly on paper and put it in an envelope. You must enclose a long self-addressed stamped envelope and 50¢.
Write to:	Fax Marketing 460 Carrollton Drive Department 97 Frederick, MD 21701
Ask for:	Flag keychains

Stuck on America

Show the world how you feel about your country by putting these flag stickers everywhere. You'll receive eight stickers to collect, stick on notebooks and folders, or give away on the Fourth of July.

Directions:	Read and follow the instructions on pages 2-8. Print your name, address, and request neatly on paper and put it in an envelope. You must enclose 75¢.
Write to:	Smiles 'N' Things P.O. Box 974 Department #1–FS Claremont, CA 91711-0974
Ask for:	Flag stickers

Red, White, and Blue

Now you can pledge allegiance to your very own flag. Wave it, stick it in your yard on national holidays, or just keep it in your room as a reminder that you live in the land of the free and the home of the brave. You'll receive one 4-by-6-inch plastic United States flag.

Directions:	Read and follow the instructions on pages 2-8. Print your request neatly on paper and put it in an envelope. You must enclose a long self-addressed stamped envelope and 50¢. Tape coins to paper or cardboard. No checks please.
Write to:	Phyllis Goodstein Department USF P.O. Box 912 Levittown, NY 11756-0912
Ask for:	U.S. flag

State Stamp Magnet

This offer is perfect for the fridge, your collection, or for those of you who want to make a statement. Choose your favorite state and you'll receive a stamp that's laminated and attached to a magnet.

Directions:	Read and follow the instructions on pages 2-8. Print your name, address, and request neatly on paper and put it in an envelope. You must enclose $1.00.
Write to:	Hicks Specialties 1308 68th Lane North Department FS97 Brooklyn Center, MN 55430
Ask for:	State stamp magnet (specify which state or District of Columbia)

State Milkcaps

Flip out over these state milkcaps. You'll receive five with a different state featured on each one. Tell your friends and trade for your favorite states.

Directions:	Read and follow the instructions on pages 2-8. Print your name, address, and request neatly on paper and put it in an envelope. You must enclose $1.00.
Write to:	Sunday International 7411 Earl Circle Huntington Beach, CA 92647
Ask for:	State milkcaps

MEADOWBROOK PRESS **1997 EDITION**

U.S. MAIL

Science and Computers

X-ray Viewer

This amazing special effects viewer not only fits in the palm of your hand, it makes your hand look X-rayed. Your bones appear to glow in rainbow colors all along your hand and arm.

Directions:	**Read and follow the instructions on pages 2-8. Print** your request **neatly** on paper and put it in an envelope. You must enclose a **long self-addressed stamped envelope** and **50¢**.
Write to:	Alvin Peters Company Empire State Plaza Department XRV P.O. Box 2400 Albany, NY 12220-0400
Ask for:	Special effects X-ray viewer

Rainbow Glasses

Surround yourself with a world full of rainbows. These glasses have holographic lenses that twist light into colorful beams all around you. You'll also receive information about light and how the glasses work.

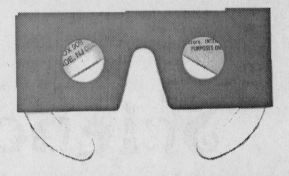

Directions:	**Read and follow the instructions on pages 2-8. Print** your request **neatly** on paper and put it in an envelope. You must enclose a **long self-addressed stamped envelope** and **$1.00**.
Write to:	Mr. Rainbows P.O. Box 908 Department FS–33 Rio Grande, NJ 08242
Ask for:	Rainbow glasses

Science Weekly

Learn about science through puzzles, word games, picture games, articles, activities, and more! Each colorful issue of *Science Weekly* presents a cool new topic on seven different reading levels. Specify your grade level to get the issue especially for kids your age (grade levels K-8).

Directions:	**Read and follow the instructions on pages 2-8. Print** your request **neatly** on paper and put it in an envelope. You must enclose a **long self-addressed stamped envelope.**
Write to:	Science Weekly Offer FSFK P.O. Box 70638 Chevy Chase, MD 20813-0638
Ask for:	Science Weekly *(specify grade level)*

The Sky's the Limit

Have a blast with astronomy and avoid the common frustrations of newcomers to stargazing. *Getting Started in Astronomy* contains seasonal star charts with instructions, a moon map, and a guide to finding more information. There's never been an easier way to get stars in your eyes.

Directions:	**Read and follow the instructions on pages 2-8. Print** your request **neatly** on paper and put it in an envelope. You must enclose a **long self-addressed stamped envelope.**
Write to:	Getting Started Booklet Sky Publishing P.O. Box 9111 Belmont, MA 02178-9111
Ask for:	Getting Started booklet

Amazing Experiments

The cast of public television's *Newton's Apple* have come up with all-new mind-blowing experiments you can try. All you need are things you find around the house to try these tricks and learn the science that explains how they work.

Hundreds of Projects

How much weight can a spider's web hold? Are fingerprints really different? Is your pet right- or left-handed? Does gravity pull food into our stomachs? Which paper towel is *really* the quicker picker-upper? This is just a sampling of the hundreds of ideas to investigate with science. Send for this flyer and find out more.

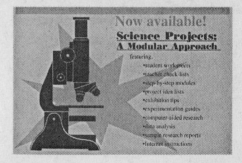

Directions:	Read and follow the instructions on pages 2-8. Print your request neatly on paper and put it in an envelope. You must enclose a long self-addressed stamped envelope.
Write to:	Newton's Apple Science Try-Its c/o Twin Cities Public Television 172 East Fourth Street St. Paul, MN 55101
Ask for:	Newton's Apple Science Try-Its

Directions:	Read and follow the instructions on pages 2-8. Print your request neatly on paper and put it in an envelope. You must enclose a long self-addressed stamped envelope.
Write to:	Applied Educational Technology P.O. Box 37 Tigerville, SC 29688
Ask for:	Science project ideas

Tricks of the Trade

Learn how to make a paper airplane do barrel rolls and fly back to you. Find out about how crystals form and learn how to make rock candy. Tease your brain with mind games, including optical illusions, jumbled words, and puzzles. Science has never been more fun!

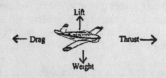

Directions:	Read and follow the instructions on pages 2-8. Print your request neatly on paper and put it in an envelope. You must enclose a long self-addressed stamped envelope and 50¢ for one trick or $1.00 for all three. Tape coins to paper or cardboard. No checks please.
Write to:	Phyllis Goodstein Department SF P.O. Box 912 Levittown, NY 11756-0912
Ask for:	Paper airplanes or Crystals and rock candy or Mind games or All three science activity sheets

The Better to See You With

Expand your mind while you enlarge your world with this miniature magnifying glass. It comes in a keychain case so you can carry it around, ready for any investigation. Or, if you're a hands-on kind of kid, send for the eyeglass repair kit instead. The handle of the magnifying glass is also a screwdriver and a place to hold the tiny screws that come with it.

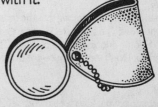

Directions:	Read and follow the instructions on pages 2-8. Print your name, address, and request neatly on paper and put it in an envelope. You must enclose $1.00.
Write to:	MKZ Enterprises 7241 West Sunrise Boulevard Department 100 Plantation, FL 33313
Ask for:	Magnifying glass or Eyeglass repair kit

Get Caught in the Web

The Internet is one of the fastest growing forms of communication today—it's also the most fun. If you have access to a computer that's hooked up to the World Wide Web, you can use the addresses below to explore everything from foreign languages, pretend cities, and games to the artwork and accomplishments of other kids. You can even contribute your own art, writing, and ideas on the Internet, which makes it a unique, ever-changing place to learn and play.

   Directions: First, you need access to a computer that is hooked up to the **World Wide Web**. There are a variety of different **online services** that provide Internet access and each one is run differently, so it's important to find out how the one you're using hooks you up to the Web.

   On this page is a list of **URLs** (uniform resource locators) that are the addresses of places on the Web. To find the cool stuff at these different addresses, you need to choose "open location" under the **File** menu at the top of your screen or go to the **Search** page of your Web browser. Type the address you want into the space provided. Usually this space will begin with "URL" and often you'll need to type over the address that is there. Web addresses always begin with "http://" which will help you identify where to type.

   Please remember as you explore that the Internet is growing and changing every day. Don't be frustrated if you can't reach a Web page right away. The sites listed here are so great that lots of people will be looking them up. Like the phone line of a popular person, some addresses may be busy. The best thing you can do is try the address later when there might be fewer people hooked up. Don't worry, there are plenty of other addresses to keep you busy!

GAMES
Playing Drool
If you could be a dog, what kind would you be? Pick your favorite and get ready for a crazy game of computer fetch.
   URL: http://www.mit.edu:8001/afs/athena.mit.edu/user/j/b/jbreiden/game/entry.html
String Figures from Around the World
View and learn how to create figures out of string. This site shows you creations from all over the world, from simple to elaborate, and explains the rich history and culture behind string figures.
   URL: http://www.ece.ucdavis.edu/~darsie/string.html

SPORTS
ESPNET SportsZone
Find out about any sport from baseball to auto racing. Look for news, stories, discussion groups, and more!
   URL: http://ESPNET.SportsZone.com

LANGUAGES
Human Languages Page
This site will direct you to places on the Web where you can learn any foreign language you like, from over sixty options.
   URL: http://www.willamette.edu/~tjones/Language-Page.html

Learn Spanish
Learn Mexican Spanish with online worksheets, tests, vocabulary, and pronunciation guides for beginners.
> **URL:** http://www.willamette.edu/~tjones/Spanish/Spanish-main.html

Learn Italian
Learn the basics of Italian with this online lesson plan, complete with vocabulary, pronunciation, exercises, and more!
> **URL:** http://www.willamette.edu/~tjones/languages/Italian/Italian-lesson.html

CULTURES

Native Web
Find out about the world's native cultures through stories, prayers, geography, languages, and a wide range of fascinating stuff.
> **URL:** http://web.maxwell.syr.edu/nativeweb/

Native Events Calendar
Find out more about the native people who live in your own area of the world. This site tells you what's happening all over the globe and gives you hints about how to respectfully participate in these events.
> **URL:** http://www.dorsai.org/~smc/native/evntmain.html

American Memory
Find out about American history through articles, photos, films, and more.
> **URL:** http://rs6.loc.gov/amhome.html

The African American Mosaic
Explore African American history and culture at this site. You'll find pictures, sound clips, text, and lists of places to find out more.
> **URL:** http://lcweb.loc.gov/exhibits/African.American/intro.html

COOL PLACES

Sea World/Busch Gardens
Whether you've visited these places or not, you will love the Web site. Learn about all kinds of animals, watch videos, or just explore the many attractions of both parks.
> **URL:** http://www.bev.net/education/SeaWorld/homepage.html

Niagara FallsCam Home Page
At this site you can actually watch a video of the falls in action! You'll also be able to learn all about the Niagara area.
> **URL:** http://FallsCam.niagara.com/

JUST FOR KIDS

Interesting Places for Kids
Play games, visit museums, learn about arts and crafts, or find other Web pages created by kids.
> **URL:** http://www.crc.ricoh.com/people/steve/kids.html

KID List
Even the name of this site is fun: KID stands for Kid's Internet Delight. At this site, you'll find lists and connections to some of the coolest Web pages around, like the Hall of Dinosaurs, Horse Country, and International Cool Kids.
> **URL:** http://www.clark.net/pub/journalism/kid.html

MUSIC

The Internet Underground Music Archive

If you're tired of hearing the same old music on the radio, check out the underground music scene at this Web site. You'll find information, discussion groups, audio clips, and pictures of musicians who play every type of music you can think of.

URL: http://www.iuma.com/

The Ultimate Band List

No matter what your favorite types of music are, you'll find lots of cool stuff at this site, from song samples and pictures to Web pages of your favorite popular performers and groups.

URL: http://american.recordings.com/wwwofmusic/ubl/ubl.shtml

ART & LITERATURE

Art Crimes: The Writing on the Wall

This site will blow your mind with images of and information about graffiti art from all over the world.

URL: http://www.gatech.edu/desoto/graf/Index.Art_Crimes.html

Children's Literature Web Guide

Find out about some of the best children's books around today and maybe even read some stories online.

URL: http://www.ucalgary.ca/dkbrown/index.html

Tales of Wonder

Read folk and fairy tales from all over the world. You'll find stories grouped according to place, so you can look up the area you're interested in and read the tales the people who live there have to share.

URL: http://www.ece.ucdavis.edu/~darsie/tales.html

Realist Wonder Society

Fairy tales, fables, art, poetry, online journals, Disney screenplays—if you like to read, you'll spend hours at this site.

URL: http://www.exploratorium.edu

SCIENCE

ExploraNet

If you have a science question, this Web site will have the answer. You'll not only be able to send in your own questions, you'll find cool pictures and information about science questions you never thought to ask.

URL: http://www.exploratorium.edu

The Franklin Institute Science Museum

Explore the past, present, and future of science and technology at this online science museum.

URL: http://www.fi.edu

Spacelink

Wow! This site is packed with cool space stuff. You'll find information about space shuttle missions, interactive field trips, satellite pictures, NASA educational programs, and the list goes on!

URL: http://spacelink.msfc.nasa.gov

INDEX

INDEX

More Books Kids Will Love!

A Bad Case of the Giggles
selected by Bruce Lansky
illustrated by Stephen Carpenter

Nothing motivates your children to read more than a book that makes them laugh. That's why this book will turn your kids into poetry lovers. Every poem included in this book had to pass the giggle test of over 600 school children. This anthology collects the royal court of children's poets (court jesters all), Shel Silverstein, Jack Prelutsky, Judith Viorst, Jeff Moss, and Bruce Lansky. The American Booksellers Association has chosen this book as "Pick of the Lists" for children's poetry.   **order #2411**

Kids Pick the Funniest Poems
compiled by Bruce Lansky
illustrated by Stephen Carpenter

Three hundred elementary kids will tell you that this book contains the funniest poems for kids—because they picked them! Not surprisingly, they chose many of the funniest poems ever written by favorites like Shel Silverstein, Jack Prelutsky, Jeff Moss, and Judith Viorst (plus poems by lesser-known writers that are just as funny). This book is guaranteed to please children aged 6–12!   **order #2410**

Girls to the Rescue
selected by Bruce Lansky

A collection of 10 folk and fairy tales featuring courageous, clever, and determined girls from around the world. This groundbreaking book will update traditional fairy tales for girls aged 8–12.   **order #2215**

"An enjoyable, much-needed addition to children's literature
that portrays female characters in positive, active roles."
                —Colleen O'Shaughnessy McKenna, author of
                    Too Many Murphys

Order Form

Quantity	Title	Author	Order No.	Unit Cost	Total
	Bad Case of the Giggles	Lansky, Bruce	2411	$15.00	
	Dads Say the Dumbest Things!	Lansky/Jones	4220	$6.00	
	Free Stuff for Kids, 1997 edition	Free Stuff Editors	2190	$5.00	
	Familiarity Breeds Children	Lansky, Bruce	4015	$7.00	
	Girls to the Rescue	Lansky, Bruce	2215	$3.95	
	Girls to the Rescue #2	Lansky, Bruce	2216	$3.95	
	Kids' Holiday Fun	Warner, Penny	6000	$12.00	
	Kids' Party Cookbook	Warner, Penny	2435	$12.00	
	Kids' Party Games and Activities	Warner, Penny	6095	$12.00	
	Kids Pick the Funniest Poems	Lansky, Bruce	2410	$15.00	
	Moms Say the Funniest Things!	Lansky, Bruce	4280	$6.00	
	New Adventures of Mother Goose	Lansky, Bruce	2420	$15.00	
	Poetry Party	Lansky, Bruce	2430	$12.00	
				Subtotal	
			Shipping and Handling (see below)		
			MN residents add 6.5% sales tax		
				Total	

YES, please send me the books indicated above. Add $2.00 shipping and handling for the first book and 50¢ for each additional book. Add $2.50 to total for books shipped to Canada. Overseas postage will be billed. Allow up to four weeks for delivery. Send check or money order payable to Meadowbrook Press. No cash or C.O.D.'s please. Prices subject to change without notice. **Quantity discounts available upon request.**

Send book(s) to:

Name _____ Phone _____

Address _____

City_____ State_____ Zip _____

Payment via:

❏ Check or money order payable to Meadowbrook Press. (No cash or C.O.D.'s please) Amount enclosed $_____

❏ Visa (for orders over $10.00 only)   ❏ MasterCard (for orders over $10.00 only)

Account #_____ Signature_____ Exp. Date _____

A FREE Meadowbrook Press catalog is available upon request.
You can also phone us for orders of $10.00 or more at 1-800-338-2232.

Mail to: Meadowbrook, Inc., 18318 Minnetonka Blvd., Deephaven, MN 55391

(612) 473-5400   Toll-Free 1-800-338-2232   FAX (612) 475-0736